A LOST HEART

ALSO BY HEATHER BLANTON

Grace Be a Lady

Hell-Bent on Blessings

A Scout for Skylar

Locket Full of Love

Carolina Homecoming

A Good Man Comes Around

Burning Dress Ranch

A Distant Heart

Romance in the Rockies

A Lady in Defiance

Hearts In Defiance

A Promise In Defiance

Daughter of Defiance

A Destiny in Defiance

Hope in Defiance

A Reckoning in Defiance

In Time For Christmas: A Novella

A LOST HEART

A SWEET WESTERN CHRISTIAN ROMANCE

BURNING DRESS RANCH
BOOK TWO

HEATHER BLANTON

A Lost Heart
Paperback Edition

CKN Christian Publishing
An Imprint of Wolfpack Publishing
1707 E. Diana Street
Tampa, FL 33610

www.cknchristianpublishing.com

First edition published in 2021.

Paperback ISBN 979-8-89567-842-8
Ebook ISBN 979-8-89567-841-1

A LOST HEART

CHAPTER ONE

She couldn't take this much longer.

Sierra Caldwell had heard all the stuffy political or society gossip she could bear. She was twenty, not forty, and ached to excuse herself from the dinner reception for the attorney general. The soft murmur of voices interlaced with the tinkling of silverware and crystal glasses reminded her that the evening would go on and on.

She nodded politely and *Uh-hmmed* her way through boring conversations about the state legislature, exorbitant tax bills, and which congressman was trading favors with which businessman. The moment she finished her dessert, she glanced at her father at the head of the table. He had his hand partly over his face, muffling his conversation as he leaned toward the attorney general.

Not that anyone could hear them over the other dozen people at the table, going on and on with their inane conversations.

At least he was engrossed in his conversation. Sierra

quietly excused herself from the two elderly gentlemen seated on each side of her and made a beeline for the stable.

HER FATHER WOULD KILL her for coming to the barn in her new gown, but she needed the smell of horses and hay to clear her nostrils of the scent of cigars and lobster bisque. She stopped at Cleopatra's stall door and smiled dreamily at the magnificent palomino, golden and glimmering like an Egyptian sand dune. The mare grumbled a welcome to Sierra, the message in her dark eyes inviting her to visit.

Sierra glanced down the breezeway to her left and then to her right. All the stable hands were gone for the night. The lights had been turned low, waiting for the final check of the night, at which point they would be snuffed. She would be gone before then. No one would know she'd ever been here.

Her father had forbidden her to groom the horses. She was only allowed to train or ride them. But Sierra loved the bond one could form with a horse by simply brushing it, and she missed the task. She used to do it all the time, before he'd married the countess.

Where was the fun in life if you didn't break the rules now and again?

She slipped inside the stall with Cleopatra and plucked a brush from the grooming bucket hanging up on the wall. "There's my gorgeous queen," she whispered, dragging the bristles down her muscular neck. "How about a ride in the morning, Your Highness?"

Cleopatra offered her a soft pucker of her lips as if the idea appealed to her.

She was a stunning horse, and one of the most intelligent Sierra had worked with yet. "I thought about selling you, Cleo, but it turns out Shebar has received an offer."

The horse grumbled again and side-stepped quickly away from her.

"Cleopatra, what—?"

"Good God, Sierra, what are you doing?" The stall door yanked open, and Kevin Hartman, her father's lead attorney, reached in, his eyes burning, grabbed her arm, and pulled her violently from the stall. "And in your new gown, yet."

Livid, his grip hurting her, Sierra snatched her arm free and stepped back from the young man in the tailored tuxedo. "How dare you lay a hand on me!" She dropped the brush—before she threw it at his head—and rubbed her wrist where his grasp had been unnecessarily savage.

A smirk lifted Kevin's lips. He pushed a lock of wavy, blond hair off his forehead and slammed the stall door. "Your father has given me permission to treat you as I see fit. Since we're to be married—"

"We are not getting married." How many times did she have to say this to her father and Kevin?

Kevin chuckled, but the humor in his golden-brown eyes was cold and sinister. He took a step toward her, and Sierra forced herself to stay still, to hide the fear that tried to surface in her expression. He glanced around the quiet, empty barn. "You shouldn't be down here alone. It's not safe."

For a moment, something hung in the air between them. An imagined threat? Or was it real?

He raised an eyebrow. "As for not marrying me, you don't seem to understand you have nothing to say about it. You and I are headed to Washington in a few years."

He reached out and touched her cheek. "You'll make a fine senator's wife."

Sierra slapped his hand away. "You could be headed to the White House and I wouldn't marry you." *God forbid, I pray I never have to marry this man.*

Again, that maddening smirk appeared that made her want to smack him unconscious. He motioned to the breezeway. "I should get you back to the party. I'll keep your"—he looked at Cleopatra—"inappropriate behavior to myself."

THE MEMORY of Kevin's startling anger and his ridiculous, pompous attitude haunted Sierra through the next morning. As her father droned on and on across from her at his desk, she daydreamed about five minutes in the saddle. To clear her head and erase the feel of Kevin's finger on her cheek. Just a quick, soul-freeing gallop down her favorite trail to the Crazy Woman Creek. A good horse under her. A sapphire, Colorado sky above her—

"Sierra, you're not listening to me."

She blinked herself back to the moment and her father, staring at her with a mix of shock and irritation. Jason Caldwell's austere features, shaved perfectly smooth, tensed. He pushed his fingers through his silver hair and sighed. "If I would allow it, you could drive me to distraction. Now, answer my question."

"Uh…" Oh, yes. Did she know her schedule? By rote. It seemed every minute of her days the last four years had been planned down to the second. "Margaret will be here at eight-thirty to go over the menu for the dinner party Friday night. Mr. Marchon will be here at ten to show me his new collection of gowns. From which you have instructed me to pick three. One must be light blue, as that is the governor's favorite color.

"At eleven, I have my art class. From noon to three, I will be meeting with various Denver philanthropic organizations, all screened by the countess to assure us they are the appropriate constituents for best impacting your political friends. I believe she has already had Margaret draw up the support we'll be pledging." In which case, her father's secretary could handle these awful meetings herself.

Sierra continued, nudged on by her father's approving nods. "From three to five, I have a meeting with the director of the Denver Home for Abandoned and Unwed Mothers to discuss the charity horse show." She paused here, happy with at least one upcoming task. "I am delighted to announce I have a buyer for Shebar, and we'll be donating all proceeds from the sale to the home." The money would support the organization for well over a year. Managed well, maybe two.

"At six..." She stumbled. Six. Oh, of course, how could she forget?

Because she'd chosen to block it out.

"I will join you and Kevin for dinner with Senator Ridgeway—"

"All right." Her father patted the air impatiently. "All right. Good enough."

"Would you like to hear my schedule for tomorrow?" It was similarly full and just as boring. The older she got, the more social responsibility her father and stepmother hefted upon her.

"No." He settled back in his massive, burgundy

leather chair and drummed his fingers on the blotter. "I understand Kevin caught you grooming Shebar last night."

A disapproving dip formed in her brow before she could stop it. *The rat.* "No, he didn't." Which was true. She had been grooming *Cleopatra* when the overbearing, stiff-as-a-starched-petticoat lawyer tracked her down in the stable.

"Are you suggesting he's lying? You weren't grooming Shebar?"

She wrestled with floating a lie, but in the end wouldn't do it. "I was grooming Cleopat—"

"Dear Lord, girl, I've told you to let the stable boys do that. You're not ten anymore. You're twenty and the daughter of a countess. Act like it."

Sierra felt her face flush. "It's a harmless, enjoyable task."

"It is menial work. Below your station now."

Ever since her father had married Countess Josephine Athena Frederica of the Dane Rosenborgs, he'd taken to thinking of nothing but climbing the high-society ladder. And a ten-year-old tomboy had been remolded into a soft, useless debutante. Sierra didn't hate her life, exactly, but she missed the tomboy and her freedom.

Trying to do anything with the horses other than riding or training them had been relabeled a cardinal sin. But Kevin had no right whatsoever to touch her…especially in anger.

Sierra raised her chin, indignant over the event. "Did Kevin happen to mention how unacceptably rude he was to me?"

"Rude?"

"He grabbed my arm violently."

"I doubt he would have hurt you, but I have given him permission to treat you with the familiarity of an engaged couple—"

"Father!" She tossed up a hand. "For the last time, I'm not marrying him."

"You'll do as I say. You have no choice. Unless you'd like to run away again."

Sierra used to run away at least once a week just after her father married the countess. For two years, she'd fought the union and the suffocating societal bonds it had brought with it. But the life of high society had eventually lulled Sierra into a brainless fog. Pretty dresses, shopping sprees, parties. For a while, she'd enjoyed the silliness of being young and wealthy. She didn't realize she'd become a pawn. A prize. A trophy.

But thanks to Kevin and that malignant look in his eyes last night, she'd snapped out of her Lotus-flower haze.

The ember of her anger still aglow, she rose to her feet, but she would not pursue the argument at the moment. She needed to think. Besides, she had more important business.

"Before your day for me begins, Father, I have an appointment. Harvey Fenton is coming to pay for Shebar."

"Fenton?" Her father's mood changed on a dime. "He's the buyer? That's excellent news. He's well-connected."

"Yes, I'm sure within minutes it will be all over Denver what philanthropic souls the Caldwells are."

"There is no reason, young lady, a charitable contribution can't benefit the giver as well as the recipient."

"And it absolutely must do both, or we'll pass on the opportunity."

"Your insolence is unbecoming."

"Your blind ambition is nauseating."

He lurched to his feet, slapping his desk. "I've had about all I'm going to take from you, young lady. Get out." He pointed at the door. "I'll let Kevin teach you some manners. Clearly, I have failed to do so."

CHAPTER TWO

"MANNERS!" SIERRA FUMED AS SHE STRODE TOWARD Shebar's stall. "I'll show them both some manners." *If he thinks I'm going to marry Kevin...well, just maybe I will run away again. Anything would be better than spending the rest of my life with the cold, calculating lawyer.*

Sierra closed her eyes and breathed in the scent of hay and leather and horse. Almost instantly, her anger began to seep away. She drifted her fingers lightly over Shebar's stall gate, worn smooth by the horse's leaning. The smells, the place, the comforting feel of the wood restored some of her peace.

Dear Lord, I believe it's going to be all right, she prayed, and then opened her eyes. The stallion stood in the center of his stall, black as a midnight sky, glistening like a still lake beneath a winter moon. The diamond-shaped blaze on his nose, a pristine white, begged for a touch. "You are beautiful, Shebar." Sierra let herself into the stall and rubbed the horse's face with affection. "I'm selling you today, boy. Don't take it personally. The money is going to a good cause. You're the down payment on the new home for abandoned women." She leaned her head against his. "My father wants to sell me to the highest bidder, too. Only I think you're going to be treated a lot better."

"Miss Caldwell?"

A man's voice echoed down the barn's breezeway and Sierra gasped. Fear and excitement jolted her heart. She couldn't wait to present this check for Shebar to the home. "I'm here, Mr. Fenton." She brushed down her split skirt and rushed out into the breezeway. Ready to greet the buyer, she was surprised to see the silhouette of two men strolling toward her. The slender outline of the man in a top hat with the cane, she knew: the potential buyer, Mr. Fenton.

The other silhouette she didn't recognize. He was tall, solid, and walked with an easy-going swagger, which seemed to add width to his already broad shoulders. Both men pulled off their hats when they saw her. "Miss Caldwell." The light from the morning sun behind them faded and they came into focus. Mr. Fenton extended his hand. "It's good to see you. I hope you don't mind, I brought a…a friend of a friend, you could say."

Sierra extended her hand to a man with a pair of stunning blue eyes looking out of a tanned, weathered face. Wavy, dark brown hair, a little unkempt, touched his collar. He was handsome but a bit rough. Or perhaps she'd simply been socializing with too many lawyers and politicians lately.

He hugged his gray hat to his chest and shook her hand firmly. "Miss Caldwell. It's nice to meet you. Henry here says you have some nice horses."

"Some of the finest. And who might you be?"

"Oh, I'm Nick Bannister. I'm the head wrangler for Burning Dress Ranch up in Wyoming."

"Miss Caldwell, I hope you won't mind, but I brought Nick along at a request from my business partner. Ranching is a new venture for me, and he suggested Nick could help with the selection of a basic remuda."

"Of course, I don't mind."

"Nick, Miss Caldwell's Arabian, Shebar, has an outstanding pedigree. As I've told you, I believe I can build the foundation of a fine herd with him."

Mr. Bannister's face tightened a touch, and instantly Sierra got a sinking feeling. "Let's have a look, then," he said.

Uneasy, she motioned further down the breezeway. "I'll bring him out to the corral for you."

"Very good." Mr. Fenton nodded, and he and Mr. Bannister walked back the way they'd come.

Sierra snatched the lunge line off the hook outside the stall and fastened it to Shebar. "I don't know who he is, boy, but I think we need to impress the socks off him."

THE STALLION WAS A GOOD HORSE, willing, steady, and he liked showing off. He pranced around the corral with panache. Sierra stood in the center of the ring and couldn't help but grin as Shebar excelled at the verbal commands. She didn't even use a lunge whip now. His coat shimmering in the high noon sun, he moved about like a dream. Any ranch would be fortunate to have him.

"Questions, gentlemen?" she asked as she waved her hand, and Shebar obediently altered his path and walked up to her. Sierra took the reins and stepped into the saddle. Both men were grinning and nodding, but Mr. Bannister still regarded her with a look of...reservation.

Shebar shifted beautifully from a walk to a trot to an easy canter, his mane and tail flying gracefully like sails in the wind. "He's got a seat comfortable as your grandmother's rocking chair. He can go at a steady canter all day before he's even tired." With a gentle tug on the leather, she slowed him back down to a walk. "He's bold and high-spirited. Fearless, I would dare say."

As she talked, she could see the stars in Mr. Fenton's eyes, but a decidedly different look in Mr. Bannister's. Doubt. Misgivings. She decided to address his concerns. She pulled Shebar up and walked him over to the men hanging on the fence. "He's fast, Mr. Bannister. Like the wind. Has the endurance of five horses. And a proven stud record."

Mr. Bannister exchanged an uncomfortable look with Mr. Fenton. "You asked me to come along so I could share my opinion."

"Yes, and I thought seeing the animal might assuage your doubts."

"Doubts?" Sierra said a bit too sharply.

Mr. Bannister flinched under her tone and sighed. "Look, ma'am, he's a fine animal. I mean, he's a thing of beauty. But he's wrong for a ranch." He patted the air apologetically. "At least for now."

Sierra's blood started rising to a boil. Who was this naysayer wrecking her plans? "He'd be a fine contribution to any stable. At any time."

With a raised brow, Mr. Fenton cut his eyes at Mr. Bannister, as if waiting for the counter-argument.

"All due respect, Fenton here isn't opening a stable. He's trying to start a ranch. Shebar is fast, agile, and has mounds of endurance. But he's spindly and hot-tempered."

"Spindly?" Sierra almost choked on the word.

"Yes, ma'am, spindly when you compare him to a good quarter horse or even some of the Spanish mustangs we've got around. Mr. Fenton needs to round up some good working horses to get started."

"Shebar can work as hard as any quarter horse or mustang or—or—whatever horse you need on a *ranch*." Her cheeks were hot and getting hotter. "What makes you such an expert on horses? Especially ones with outstanding bloodlines?" This cowboy might know mutts and mustangs, but he didn't know true quality. She raised her chin proudly. "We can trace Shebar's lines all the way back to Sheik Moussaf El Adani of Arabia."

Mr. Bannister gave her a blank look. An expression totally unreadable to Sierra. Then he turned and faced Mr. Fenton. "You want to run a ranch or do horse shows?"

Mr. Fenton pursed his lips and nodded. "I understand. And this is why I asked you to come along. Miss Caldwell, I am sorry. Shebar is a beautiful animal, but..."

Sierra wanted to kick Mr. Bannister in the shin. What had he done? Why was he sabotaging this sale? "Apparently, Mr. Fenton"—she slid a hot gaze over to Mr. Bannister—"you need a short, stocky, ugly animal to move cattle."

Mr. Bannister's lips twitched into a smug smile. "You got any of those?"

NICK LET out a tense whistle as he and Fenton climbed up into the man's barouche. "She sure took that personal," he mused aloud. Snooty, rich, society gals were so high-strung. "Like she's royalty or something, and how dare I question her."

Fenton chuckled and ordered his driver home. Then he muttered, "Royalty or something." As the carriage rolled toward the city of Denver, four miles in the distance, he spoke with regret obvious in his tone. "Sierra Caldwell has some of the finest horses in the state."

"Yes, she does. If you're into fox hunting and jumping ivy-covered fences." He raised his eyebrows at Fenton. "Ranching is a different world. You sure you want to step into it?"

The man rested his hands on top of his cane and drummed his fingers. "You've left me no choice. I'll be ostracized by the finest circles of society for daring to question Sierra's horses."

Nick frowned, trying to determine if Fenton was joking or not. "That would be a shame."

Fenton narrowed his eyes at him. "Look, I understand why we didn't buy the horse. I feel as if you offered sage advice. Pretty horses later. For now, what you call cow ponies is what I need. Yes?"

"Yes."

"Your brother said I was fortunate you were in town. I think he was right. You just saved me ten thousand dollars."

Nick's eyes bugged. "She wanted ten thousand dollars for the stallion? Do you know how many cattle you can buy for money like that?"

Fenton smirked. "I was cornered by her at a party and swayed by her beauty. You slapped me back to earth."

Nick whistled again and settled deeper in the seat. Green eyes. Strawberry-blonde hair. Nice curves. And flawless, pink cheeks that flushed an enticing shade of red. Yeah, he wasn't blind. Sierra Caldwell was pretty, but— "Not ten thousand dollars worth of pretty," he mumbled. "I ever want to spend ten thousand dollars on a nag just because some gal smiles at me…I hope somebody slaps *me* back to earth."

"I hope I'm around to oblige."

CHAPTER THREE

THE TRAIN STATION WAS UNUSUALLY CROWDED, AND WHAT little good cheer Sierra had was disappearing quickly. A man carrying a large travel case in front of him hit her in the elbow as he rushed by. Stars and lightning shot up and down her arm.

"Ouch," she howled, pulling her arm close to her body and rubbing the elbow frantically.

"My goodness, this is ridiculous," Claudette Bishop complained from beside her. She was a large woman squeezed into a tight, yellow dress, and scurrying travelers seemed to bounce off her like marbles off a balloon.

Mostly. A tall man carrying a saddle bumped into her, evoking an indignant grumble from her. He apologized immediately, turned to continue on his way, when a buckle on the saddle snagged Claudette's hat, yanking it from her head and sending her hair spilling.

"Gracious," Claudette squealed and clawed for her chapeau.

Sierra started to laugh when yet another traveler

knocked her into Claudette. "You're right," she said, righting herself. "This is ridiculous."

"Now I wish we'd all simply agreed to meet on the train." Claudette tried pinning her hair back up, but her mass of curly blonde hair cascaded over her face.

"We didn't, so we'll fight this out till we're all together. Here, let me help you." Sierra set down her valise, took her friend's hat and pins, and made a valiant effort to tidy her up amid the jostling flow of humanity.

Seven other women from the Denver Ladies' Club were due any moment, and they were all taking the train to Chicago for a fundraising event. Anything to do with horses or the homeless, and Sierra could be counted on to attend or assist. The forum in Chicago revolved around fundraising techniques. An especially timely event since Shebar's sale had collapsed.

"There." Sierra was better with horse manes, but she'd put her friend back together.

"Ah, thank you," Claudette said, touching her hat and patting the hair in back. "That's such a shame about Shebar's sale falling through, but I'm sure this conference will be helpful."

"Yes," Sierra said flatly and stopped herself there. No use crying over spilled milk. Or thinking she'd like to claw out Mr. Bannister's icy blue eyes.

Claudette's hair and hat suddenly shifted of their own volition and fell over the woman's face, as if intent on annoying her. The woman puttered her lips in disgust. "You are better with horse manes, my dear, than buns. I'm going to the ladies' room."

"I'll stay here and wait for everyone."

"You do that." Claudette patted Sierra on the shoulder and disappeared into the flow of people, getting jostled and jostling in return. Like debris in a flooded river.

A porter pushing a cart piled high with steamer trunks and bags steered it carefully through the stream of bodies and parked it next to the edge of the platform. Sierra smiled politely at him just as another man with a huge case struck her between the shoulder blades, nearly knocking her off her feet. She let go a squeal and a grunt, caught as she was somewhere between pain and anger. The man never even looked back.

"Here, ma'am." The porter, a black man with skin the color of fresh coffee, gently tugged her over to his cart. "They's a team of rasslers here about. From the university. Big boys. Biggest I ever seen. They hit a little thing like you, you liable to go flying off to the moon."

Sierra chuckled at the image and nodded. "Thank you. It's wild here today."

"Yes'm. Some big political thing going on in Chicago. Lots of folks heading out. You one of them delegates?"

"No, no. I'm going to a conference to learn new ways of fundraising. I am trying to help renovate the Denver Home for Abandoned Women and Children."

The porter's eyes lit up. "My laws, what a coincidence. My sister spent some time there."

"Really? What was her name?"

"Tallulah Freeman. She was there, oh, about a year-and-a-half ago, I seem to recall."

"Oh, that was before I got involved. Was her time there helpful?"

"Yes, ma'am, but the best thing the home did for her was send her off to Burning Dress Ranch."

Sierra's jaw nearly fell open. She tightened her lips into a flat line and quickly looked away. "Burning Dress?"

"Yes, ma'am. You heard of it?"

She smiled for no other reason than to release the

expression frozen on her face. "I just recently became acquainted. I didn't know it had any business with the home." *Other than bad-mouthing my horses.* A thought which led her to wonder if Mr. Nick Bannister had sabotaged the sale of Shebar so he could sell Mr. Fenton some cow ponies. He was clearly a despicable, dishonorable man. If she ever saw him again, she would—

"My sister came back from there a new woman."

"Really?" Sierra was intrigued. Anything that helped women reclaim their lives mattered to her. "How so?"

"She learned a trade at the ranch. Now she's working at a place over in Kansas. Happy as a lark."

Sierra mused over this story. It was, after all, the intention of the Denver home to help move abandoned, unwanted, and unwed women on to better situations. Grudgingly, she admitted it sounded as if Burning Dress had done exactly that.

"Look here," the porter said, reaching into his pocket. "Tallulah sent me this. I like lookin' at it when I'm having a bad day."

He handed Sierra a postcard. On the front, it showed a large, two-story log home with a massive stone chimney. The picture had been carefully touched up with paint, creating a vibrant photograph with a bright blue sky, deep green evergreens standing guard over the house, soaring mountains in the background. Several women stood in front of the structure, all of various ethnic backgrounds, one holding the reins to a pinto. Smiling broadly, all of the ladies in the photo were young, early 20s or so…except the one with the horse.

Sierra peered closer. This woman, perhaps in her early fifties, give or take, was tall, had a regal bearing, was painted with silver hair, and stared intently into the camera. Her smile was friendly and light, yet her gaze seemed to communicate almost…a plea.

This is a place of peace and safety. The Lord welcomes you. Come and find yourself.

Sierra blinked. The surety of the thought puzzled her.

"Oh, 'scuse me, ma'am. I be right back." The porter darted off, apparently to avert some crisis.

She flipped the card over and read the brief note on the back. "Feel like I have come home. Most beautiful place I've ever lived. See you soon. Love, Tallulah."

Stars of pain exploded in Sierra's head. Her mind screeched to a halt. Scuffling sounds filled her ears, something—bodies?—slammed into her. She felt herself falling, but couldn't pull thoughts together fast enough to react. Her forehead impacted with an immovable object, and a black fog rolled over her…

"Oh, gee, miss!" A young man's voice filtered into Sierra's foggy brain. Hands slipped under her arms. "Holy cow, help me, boys." She felt the hands lift her to her feet. She blinked, but her focus was slow in coming, and her head rang with pain. She realized someone had hold of her elbow, and possibly there was an arm around her.

"Miss, I am so sorry. Are you all right?"

Was she? She pressed her fingers to her throbbing forehead. "I'm fine," she mumbled without thought.

"Oh, boy," another young man said. "Let's get her on her train so she can sit down."

"Yeah. Miss, can we put you on your train? Is this one it?"

"Where you headed?" another voice asked.

Sierra heard the words but couldn't make sense out of them. Where was she headed? She blinked again, still trying to clear her vision. She could only make out a blur of faces and motion. She felt surrounded, but not threatened.

"Here. She dropped this."

"What is—oh, hey, looks like she's going to Wyoming. Is that right, miss?" a blurry face asked. "Are you going to…to Burning Dress Ranch in Wyoming?"

Burning Dress. The lady with the intense stare. *This is a place of peace and safety. Come here and find yourself.* "Yes, the ranch."

"Burning Dress?"

"Burning Dress," she repeated, still attempting to focus.

"All right, we'll get you to your seat."

"We're gonna miss our train," one of the boys whined.

"No, we won't. Quit being a baby. Grab her bag."

The pounding in Sierra's head was fading, but she was still confused, a little nauseated, and wobbly as a new colt. The arm around her tightened, and she could tell a person of some bulk had her.

"Come on, miss. Least we can do is get you squared away so you don't miss your train."

Oh, yes, that sounded fine. She was eager to sit down.

As if she were looking down a tunnel, she saw the toes of her lace-up boots moving, the blue lace at the bottom of her dress flicking outward with each step. A short stool appeared. With assistance, she climbed it and then was walking down the aisle of a train. Her guide eased her into a seat. "All right, miss."

Sierra took a deep breath, blinked, intent on clearing her vision, and looked up. A young man with short-cropped, blond hair and broad shoulders smiled down at her. "I sure am sorry for plowing you over like that. We've got you on the train. You can take it easy from here."

"Come on, Jack. We're gonna have to run to catch *our* train," a voice said from behind the boy.

He frowned, stared into Sierra's eyes, as if he had a moment of doubt. "You are going to Burning Dress Ranch, right? You were standing right next to the train."

A question. She wasn't sure of the answer. Instead, she repeated, "Burning Dress Ranch." The words were stuck in her head.

The young man nodded and stepped back. "Then safe travels, miss. A couple of stops and then you'll be there." He touched his forehead, as if tapping the brim of an invisible hat, and hurried out of Sierra's fuzzy vision.

"A couple of stops," she mumbled and sank into the seat for blessed sleep.

CHAPTER FOUR

Nick dismounted and wrapped his reins around the hitching post. The train had just pulled into the station, and before he'd walked up on the platform, folks were spilling out. A few hadn't bothered to wait for the porter, but jumped out ahead of him and took off running. Nick ambled along through the increasing flow of passengers, nodding at the folks he recognized. He was on his way to the last car, the one with livestock.

"Hey, Nick."

He turned at the sound of his name. His pard, Hub, leaned against the train station and flashed him a broad smile—all white and toothy. The kind that made the gals at Big Nose Bob's Saloon fall all over themselves to wait on him. They called him Handsome Hub. He had shiny, wavy, blonde hair and a stout build, and he never passed up a chance to flirt with a female.

At least he was a hard worker. He never shirked it, Nick was pleased to say. "Let's unload 'em into the corral. Give 'em a chance to calm down before we move them."

Hub pushed off the wall and tipped his hat saucily. "Sounds like a plan, pard. Any of them worth ten thousand dollars?" He flashed that toothy grin again.

Nick had told Hub about Sierra Caldwell and how fine her horses were. Good-looking animals, just not fit for ranching. "Nah. Just some healthy grade horses. Four mares and a gelding." Funny how the girl had sort of stayed on his mind these past couple of weeks. He slapped his thigh, surprised at his distraction. "Dang, forgot my rope. Let me—" He turned, intent on double-timing it back to his horse when he saw her, and his mind froze, his feet locked up, and he felt his jaw slip open.

Sierra Caldwell was standing twenty feet away, talking to Buddy, the depot manager. "It's her," he whispered.

Hub came to attention like a dog with a scent. "Who?" He tracked Nick's gaze. "The gal? You know her?"

"What?" Nick blinked himself back to the moment. "No. I thought I did." He waved the idea away—as far as Hub was concerned. "Let me get my rope and I'll meet you at the last car."

Hub hesitated, gave the girl a good once-over, but then shrugged and strode off toward the appointed spot.

Nick ambled in her direction, intending to pass just close enough to get a good look. If it were her, he would apologize for insulting her horses, but not for his opinion. Or maybe he wouldn't say anything at all to the Queen of Sheba. Maybe he would just walk right on by her, like he didn't recall that pretty face and all that strawberry-blonde hair spilling down her shoulders.

"I think I'm supposed to go to Burning Dress Ranch."

"Burning Dress, huh," Buddy repeated. The old man

cast about and dropped his gaze like a hammer on Nick. "Hey, just the man we need to see. Come here, Nick."

The choice taken away from him, Nick raised his chin and strode up to the pair, giving her a good look at his face. "Howdy, ma'am." The lack of recognition in her face puzzled him.

"Glad we caught ya. This here lady needs a ride out to Burning Dress."

Nick was caught off guard. "You?"

"Me?"

"Says she's had some kind of an accident, can't remember anything. 'Cept she thinks she's supposed to go out to Burning Dress."

"Accident, huh?" He tried to smile without making it come across like a smirk. What kind of game was she playing?

Jade eyes drilled into him, but still no flicker of recognition lit in them. Puzzled, Nick dragged his hat off. "You're serious? You don't remember m—anything?"

She waved a postcard in front of him. "I'm wondering if I know Tallulah. Or if I'm Tallulah."

"You're definitely not Tallulah. Seeing as how Tallulah is a tall, Black woman who left Burning Dress a few months ago."

Her chin came up in that hoity-toity way. "I don't think this is very funny, and I don't appreciate you making light of my situation."

She hadn't forgotten her blue blood ways, he saw. Society gals never did take jokes well. Not that he knew a lot of them. His hackles up, he jutted out his hand. "I'm Nick Bannister. I work at the ranch. And believe me, I would be most happy to give you a lift, Miss..."

She didn't take his hand and huffed softly in disgust. "Weren't you listening? I don't know."

He scratched his eyebrow to hide his irritation at her tone. "Well, uh, how about we call you, oh, Princess, for the time being."

She wrinkled her nose. "Princess?"

"Yeah, as in, Your Royal Highness."

"I don't think I like that any better." She passed a suspicious glare over him, as if she was beginning to suspect his dislike.

He dropped his hat back in place. "Just until we can figure out something better."

"'Fore you leave, there's a matter of her ticket. From Denver." Buddy extended his hand, palm up.

Nick cut his eyes at the princess, who once again shrugged in a dismissive way. "I'm sorry. I'm sure I can pay you or your employer back...soon."

He reached for some coins in his pocket. "Yeah, you'll pay me back."

The ticket settled, he started walking down the depot toward Hub. Turned out he wouldn't need his rope.

"Should I follow you?" she asked.

"If you want a ride out to the ranch," he answered without looking back. An instant later, she was beside him, trying to keep up with the pace set by his long stride. He pointed ahead at a wagon heavily loaded with supplies. "Ride in the back."

She shot him a quick scowl, studied the wagon for a moment, noted the bench seat loaded with packages, and huffed. But without another word, she walked over and began to climb up into the back. Hub walked over to Nick just then and motioned to her. "Who's that? Didn't know we were picking anybody up today."

"Yeah, surprised me, too. Listen"—he tapped Hub in the gut—"go see if Walt down at the livery will give you a hand with these horses. I need to get Her Ladyship out to the ranch pronto."

"Sure." Hub studied the girl for a moment, a sly little grin playing around his lips. "She's not hard on the eyes."

"Guess not. Go on now."

"Yeah." Hub blinked. "Say, I don't need any help with just six horses."

"Suit yourself." Nick started walking toward the wagon and nearly stopped when Sierra Caldwell looked up at him with the clear intent of murder.

"Look at this." She held part of her skirt up, an ugly tear about three inches long slicing across the blue lace. "Why am I sitting back here with barbed wire?"

He climbed into the wagon, shoved a package wrapped in brown paper over a few inches to make room for himself, and grabbed the reins. "'Cause the front seat is full."

Tickled with the chance for a little harmless humbling of Her Ladyship, he released the brake and slapped the reins.

THE LATE AFTERNOON sun sent long, dark shadows stretching across the hilly plain. Nick looked off in the distance and caught sight of some of the crew moving a small herd down to Fat Man Mesa for water.

He and Her Highness had been in the wagon for over an hour, and she hadn't uttered a word. He had only volunteered that the ranch was a two-hour ride. She had grunted in that don't-bother-me-peasant way. Oh, that made his blood boil. He was supposed to believe she didn't know who the heck she was...but wiping her brain had still left a haughty spirit behind?

He wasn't sure he bought this charade. Yet, she sure had looked at him without a whit of recognition. Could she be that above things? Not remembering the faces of the lowly *help*? Maybe she was *pretending* not to have any memory, but also, maybe she literally didn't remember him? It was all too confusing and highly suspect in his book.

Nah. He wasn't buying the cockamamy charade. She might not remember Nick, but she knew exactly who she was.

And he wasn't inclined to forget about her calling his cow ponies short, stocky, and ugly. Yep, the comment hadn't endeared the princess to him. Much less her high-and-mighty attitude about the Arabian. That was no horse for real cattle work, but he didn't owe her or anybody—well, except Fenton—an explanation.

He glanced back at her several times. She was trying to keep her bum on the sack of flour and her dress away from the rolls of barbed wire, all while the wagon was jolting and skipping on the rutted road like a Mexican jumping bean. Her expression vacillated between annoyance and...worry. Subtle differences, but he saw them. Unexpectedly, his conscience stung him a little.

She was a high society gal raised with the finer things. She could have better manners, but maybe she'd never had anybody correct her. And he had been a little harsh about her horses. They were fine animals. Especially Shebar.

He cleared his throat and came up with the words for a peace offering. "I suppose I could move some of these packages up here—"

"I'm fine." She tucked her skirt behind her legs and stuck her nose in the air. "Fine. Just fine."

Well, see if I ask again... He slapped the reins and moved the horses up to a faster pace.

WHEN THEY PULLED up in front of the main house, he watched her compare the postcard in her hand to the beautiful log home before them. "Did you think I wasn't bringing you to the right place?"

She scowled at him. "I was just looking—" She bit that off and gazed out over the ranch, busy with cowgirls and horses moving to and fro, chickens skittering wildly out of the way. A group of women in a wagon rode in from the opposite side of the yard and stopped at the barn. Some were in pants. Some in split skirts, a couple in bloomers. All of them were carrying hoes and shovels.

"That's the farm crew," he said as he pulled up the brake. He saw the question form in her eyes. "Yep, it's all women here. Just a few men."

"I don't understand."

"I reckon you will." He jumped down. "I'll take you to Miss Sally. She'll explain everything."

CHAPTER FIVE

SALLY ROSE AT THE KNOCK ON HER DOOR. "COME."

Nick drifted in, a hesitation in his movements that she noted immediately. Behind him, a young girl stalked his footsteps. A pretty thing, in her early twenties, with the most beautiful head of strawberry blond hair Sally had ever seen. The blue-green of her dress was perfect for her eyes—eyes which immediately reflected back an odd emptiness. With an edge. There was something... haughty in the way she held her head, her chin up a touch too high.

"Nick. Good to see you. What have you brought me?"

"Got a little bit of a strange situation here, Miss Sally. This young lady got off the train and said she's supposed to be here."

Sally tilted her head a little to the right and tossed her long, silver braid over her shoulder, assessing the girl more openly.

"You don't know me?" the mysterious guest said.

"Should I?"

"I don't know."

DISMISSING NICK, Sally gave the girl a moment to settle into the wingback chair before her desk, and survey the office. The warm mixture of rustic elements, such as the gun rack and Indian weapons on the log walls, mirrored the culture of Wyoming. The house had a feminine side as well, though, with its velvet curtains and strategically placed ferns and flowers.

"All right, young lady." Sally laced long, elegant fingers together and rested her hands in her lap. "Explain yourself."

The girl shrugged. "I can't. I came-to on the train and was told I was headed to Burning Dress Ranch in Wyoming. I don't remember anything before that."

"Came-to? I'm sorry. Back the wagon up and start again." Wearing pants, Sally pulled a booted foot up on her leg and clutched her ankle. "This is a heck of a story."

"I know. I woke up on the train. I had a postcard in my hand from someone named Tallulah from Burning Dress Ranch."

"Tallulah? Did she send you here?"

"I have no idea."

Well, if this wasn't the most perplexing thing. Sally flicked her eyes heavenward. *Sent me a mystery, have You, Lord?* "So, until the moment you opened your eyes on a train headed out of Denver—you don't have any memories of anything else?"

For the first time, the icy edge Sally had seen in the girl's face faltered. "No. I hoped once I made it here… that you…that something would be familiar." Her chin trembled and she sniffled. "It's quite unnerving, but I hoped this place would explain everything."

Sally's heart went out to the girl. How lost she must feel, and she was trying so hard to keep a brave face. "Do you know anything about Burning Dress? What we do here?"

"No. I did notice the women. Nearly every one I've seen is female."

"Burning Dress is a special place. Women come here…for second chances. There are no handouts. Only a hand up." By the pinch in the girl's brow, Miss Sally could see she didn't know how that applied to her. For that matter, neither did Miss Sally. "Let's start with the basics." She slid her Bible toward her. "I suspect you can read, but let's make sure."

The girl took the Book, looked questioningly at Miss Sally. "Anywhere?"

"Anywhere."

She opened the book, stared at the words for a moment, then read aloud, "For there is nothing hid, which shall not be manifested, neither was any thing kept secret, but that it should come abroad."

"Well, you know how to read. You learned that somewhere."

"Yes, I suppose." She brushed her fingers over the words. "Seemed oddly appropriate, didn't it?"

Sally smiled up at heaven. "Nothing odd about it. He will speak to you if you listen with your heart."

The girl shifted uncomfortably.

There's time for that… "So, we'll figure out what else you know. In the meantime, what are we going to call you?"

The girl frowned at the question, evoking Miss Sally's curiosity. "What's that look for?"

"Your hand, Nick, suggested Princess. Or Your Royal Highness."

Sally was puzzled by this sarcastic suggestion coming from Nick, normally as polite as a Sunday school teacher. "Well, we have to call you something. If I asked you 'What is your name,' what would you say? Blurt it out."

Sierra tried. "Ssss..." Her face went blank.

"Susan? Stephanie? Scarlett?" Sally tried, prodding.

The girl shook her head. "Nothing seems right." She began hissing, trying to form a word. "Ssss...sa...rah." Light flickered in her eyes.

Sally smiled at the progress. "We'll go with Sarah... Your Royal Highness."

Sarah didn't smile. "It's not right, but it's...something."

"One of the things that happens here, Sarah, is the girls learn a trade. A way to make a living, whether they have a man in their lives or not. They can stand on their own two feet when they leave here and never have to choose a more base form of employment."

"That's commendable."

"In your case, we'll start out slow. Cast about carefully. See if you have any skills. In the meantime, I think we should have Doc look at you."

"I feel perfectly fine." She sounded almost insulted by the idea of a doctor. "I just can't remember anything."

"You have a bruise on your forehead."

Sarah touched the place. "I don't...I don't recall what—"

"A doctor is not a bad idea. We'll make sure you're well before we push you for much more."

"Very well. If you insist."

"I do." Sally smiled, softening the nonnegotiable

recommendation. "Supper is in an hour. I'll show you to your quarters. You have time for a nap before dinner."

Sarah smoothed her hair down with a light touch. "After the horrendous ride out here with the barbed wire, a rest sounds wonderful. By the way, why is it called Burning Dress Ranch?"

Miss Sally smiled. "The short answer is because this is a place for new beginnings. I'll tell you the whole story some other time."

SALLY LEFT Sarah to get settled in her corner of the dorm and went hunting for Nick. Nothing about this situation felt right, and he was acting...odd. She found him at the corral, running a pick around his horse Dante's back hoof.

"Picked up a stone?" she asked, ambling up.

"I think so. Better than a loose shoe."

She let him work for a moment more before speaking again. "Tell me about Sarah."

"Sarah?"

"Oh, that's right." Sally laid her arms on the corral fence and gazed out at the hills succumbing quickly to twilight. "You wanted to call her, what was it? Princess? Her Ladyship?"

She saw Nick wince. He finished with the horse and dropped the leg. "Sarah is her name?"

"No. We tried guessing. Sarah didn't exactly ring a bell, but something about it she liked. So what do you know about her?"

It took him a long time to answer. He pretended to be lost in checking Dante's hooves, but Sally knew he was stalling. Why?

"She got off the train from Denver," he finally said. "I saw her on the platform talking to Buddy."

"And that's it?"

"She got off the train from Denver," he said carefully.

"Why did you suggest Princess as a name for her? I thought that was uncharacteristically rude for you."

"Aw, just something about her says snooty."

"Like a society girl?"

"Yeah, maybe. I don't know." He straightened up and ran his hand over his neck, as if the conversation was causing him stress. He hadn't looked her in the eye yet, either. Sally took note of this behavior but decided not to push. For the time being.

She folded her arms and sighed. "She could have gotten on the train in Denver or transferred trains, in which case she could be from anywhere."

Nick unwound Dante's reins from the fence and stepped back with the horse. "Anything else, ma'am?"

"No, I guess not."

He tapped the brim of his hat in goodbye, took the horse by the halter, and led him into the barn. Sally chewed thoughtfully on Nick's behavior. It didn't take a genius to see he was hiding something. *What in the world could it be, Lord? You want to let me in on things?*

She waited a moment for a revelation, but the Lord held His tongue. Maude stepped out the side door just then and commenced to ringing the life out of the dinner bell. A large, energetic woman, she did everything with vigor.

Its chime, loud and clear, signaled the end to the day. The girls working in the garden or building the new hay shed put their tools away. A line formed at the rain barrel so they could wash up quickly for supper. Others slowly drifted out of the barn or from the corral and made their way toward the house.

A few spoke, most waved as they passed Sally. She nodded and smiled at them. She knew these girls. Why they were here. What they hoped to get from Burning Dress. And what she hoped for them.

Sarah was an enigma. Nick was right about the snooty part. Something in Sarah's background said money and class. Expectations. Entitlement. At the moment, that was all Sally knew. No. One more thing.

She knew Nick knew something about the girl, too.

SARAH SAT down on the lower bunk and surveyed the dorm room. Two rows of four bunk beds filled the area. At one end, the enormous river rock fireplace offered the promise of comforting warmth on winter nights. Along the walls, between the beds, coats and various clothing hung from pegs. At the foot of each bed rested two small footlockers or chests. One for each bunk, she supposed. Each bed was covered in quilts, blankets, and often embroidered pillows. A nightstand beside them revealed a little about each resident. Family photos, books, Bibles.

The room was neat, spartan, and...well, she couldn't quite find the right word. The whole place felt *beneath* her.

Sarah hugged her valise to her. All she owned in the world. This too felt wrong...unacceptable. A strange emotion with no background or context for it.

Frustrated, she pressed a hand to her forehead. She tried to force her mind back to something other than the rock-and-sway of the train that had awakened her. The memory was intruded upon by Mr. Nick Bannister and blue eyes that she would have liked to think about under different circumstances.

Now, he merely annoyed her. In fact, she was angry with him. He was...insolent. She examined the tear in her dress. His fault. How dare he put her in the back of the wagon?

She huffed and laid back on the bed. Who am I? Where am I from? What happened to me? For some reason, these questions led her back to Miss Sally. A strange, beautiful, elegant woman who bandied about in men's trousers, yet moved with the grace of royalty. She seemed more than capable of running a ranch. The confidence the woman exuded...*comforted* Sarah. Gave her a sense of stability—

"Hello there."

Sarah gasped and sat up. A young woman with two long, red braids and a pretty face topped with a widow's peak sat on the bunk across from her, absently rolling up her sleeves.

"Sorry, didn't mean to startle you."

She spoke with an odd, almost musical cadence and heavy accent. Swedish, perhaps? Sarah wondered.

"You're new." The woman compared her sleeves, assessing to see if they were even.

Sarah almost gawked at the girl's meaty forearms. Stout enough to belong to a small man. "Yes, I guess I am."

"I am April."

She jutted out her hand, and Sarah accepted. "My," she said, flinching. "What a grip you've got." In fact, she noted the girl was of a stout build in general, especially across her chest and shoulders.

"Yes, sorry, I work with my hands. I'm the blacksmith-in-training. What are you going to do?"

"I don't know."

"What do you like to do?"

"I don't know."

April's brow scrunched. "Where are you from?"

"I don't know."

"Well, what is your name?"

"I don't know that, either, but you can call me Sarah."

April screwed her lips up into a comical grimace. "What's the matter? You bump your head or something?"

"I think maybe I did."

"You can't remember anything?"

The girl's questions and abrupt manner were tiresome, but Sarah supposed she'd best get used to answering the inane questions. "I woke up on a train bringing me here, and it...seemed right. That's all I know."

A slow grin lifted the girl's lips. "I've heard some pretty strange stories when it comes to how or why girls show up at Burning Dress. Yours is maybe the strangest, *yah*?"

Sarah's curiosity sparked to life. Maybe knowledge was the key to retrieving her memory. "What is the story behind this place? Why is it mostly women running it? Who is Miss Sally?"

The clear, jarring clang of the dinner bell drifted over the ranch and April rose, grinning. "Supper. Come. I'm starved."

SARAH FOLLOWED April to a large room filled with three rows of long tables and dozens of women chattering like hens, busy eating the evening meal. Sarah flinched at the volume. Twenty-some females made a lot of noise, and she didn't like it very much. It seemed so…unrefined.

"Come." April tugged her sleeve. "I usually sit over here."

Sarah followed her to a table in the back, near the large fireplace. Several other women were already seated. April pulled a chair out for Sarah and then moved to the next open seat, one over. Between them, a girl—Oriental, Sarah noted—sat quietly eating her beans and rice. She didn't appear to have touched her pork chop.

Settled, April shot her hand into the air. She leaned around the girl and motioned for Sarah to do the same. Puzzled, it took a moment for Sarah to realize April was flagging down the servers. They responded quickly, delivering bowls of green beans, creamed corn, fried squash, and a platter of fried pork chops. Other hands further down the table went up. Sarah took a cue from April, serving herself and then passing the food in the direction of the waving hands.

Sarah's stomach grumbled greedily with the first, tasty bite of corn. The meal struck her as simple but good. She picked up her knife to cut the chop, wondering why she would label the food as simple. What did that say about her past meals? The home she was lost to, for the moment.

"You should say the blessing."

The Oriental girl beside Sarah had spoken so softly, it took a second for the words to cut through the noise in the room, and she paused her knife. "I'm sorry. Did you say something?"

The girl looked at Sarah's plate, avoiding meeting her gaze. "Miss Sally has blessed the meal. Late comers, however, should say their own blessing."

The suggestion caused Sarah to stumble for words. "A-a blessing?" She searched the black cave in her mind. For the life of her, she couldn't recall one. She felt the girl staring at her now, surreptitiously, but staring just the same. "Thank you, uh, Lord," Sarah rushed. "Thank you for this meal. Amen." She paused over the prayer. Simple…yet it had brought her a little comfort.

She completed the task of cutting her first bite of chop and glanced over at her neighbor as she mulled the flavor. *This is good. Very good.* But the girl next to her hadn't touched the meat yet. "You should try the pork chops. They're wonderful."

When she didn't respond, merely continued to push green beans around on her plate, Sarah turned to her. She was a tiny thing, frail, mostly skin and bones, but her clothes and hair were clean. Timid, beaten down, the girl's weary countenance tugged at her. Sarah doubted she'd been here long to still look so scrawny. Food didn't appear to be a problem with Burning Dress. "My name is Sarah. Are you new to the ranch?"

"Two weeks now."

"Two weeks. Oh." Sarah could only guess the state the girl had been in upon her arrival to still be so skinny.

The conversation going awkwardly, she pushed on, mostly to fill the silence. "This is April. Have you met her?"

The two flicked each other quick glances, then April offered her hand. "Yeah, you're Polly, aren't you?"

Polly shook her hand, but her grip appeared to be light and fragile, and less than enthusiastic.

"Polly?" Sarah repeated, perplexed by the Western name.

"My real name is quite difficult for Americans to pronounce." Polly spoke softly and, to compound the communication issue, her words were coated in a thick accent that Sarah struggled to decipher.

"At least you know your name," Sarah finally mumbled, assuming she'd heard correctly, and returned to her chop. The girl wasn't very conversational, perhaps for more reasons than the language barrier. Sarah didn't know, but she wasn't inclined to force polite conversation.

As she worked her way through the meal, she glanced around the room. Women of every age, weight, and background came to Burning Dress Ranch. Some were quite chatty. Others barely looked up from their plates. Like Polly.

Sarah once again looked at the girl and readied a smile, but she paid no mind. In fact, she pushed her plate away, rose, bowed quickly to everyone at the table, and then slipped away. She was puzzling, little Polly. Sarah couldn't help but wonder how she'd wound up here. Again, she studied the crew of women, looking more closely at them. Their expressions. The way they sat.

Some made eye contact with their peers. Some didn't. Some ate heartily. Some barely at all. A few seemed to purposely distance themselves at the table with hunched shoulders, downcast eyes. Miss Sally hadn't said it outright, but the ranch was more than a place for women to learn a skill. They were also recovering from a trauma of some sort, Sarah would have bet.

The idea took her gaze back to April. She wasn't manly, but she was almost as muscular as one. And she talked a lot. Women who did that were usually hiding something.

Weren't they?

The thought vexed Sarah. Why did she naturally

assume that? "April, what did you do before you came to Burning Dress?"

April's hands froze in the middle of scooping beans. Her face tensed. Sarah flinched. "I'm sorry. Obviously, I've overstepped."

April finished with the bite and shook her head. "No. Not your fault. Simple enough question. It's just that what I did was…" She set her fork down on her plate and took a long time to answer. "Well, I was rather weak and sickly. People—my husband, I mean—they didn't respect me."

Sarah understood April was answering the question without giving details. Respecting the word play, she said, "Well, you're not weak anymore. I dare say you could wrestle a bear and win."

April flexed her fingers and watched the muscles flex in her forearm. "*Yah*. Maybe."

Sarah took another bite and used the pause to think of a way to change the subject. "I wonder what Miss Sally and Mr. Bannister will have me doing tomorrow." As if summoned by her mention of him, the man entered the dining hall, scanned the room, and then strode toward something or someone. Momentarily, Miss Sally stood up, and the two leaned into each other to hear over the chatter and clink of silverware.

Sarah noted several women throughout the room watching the pair intently. Or, to be more accurate, they were watching Mr. Bannister. She twirled her fork on the plate and surveyed the man as well, trying to see him from an unbiased perspective.

He was handsome. And she did like the way the jeans accentuated his muscular thighs. His shape was not unpleasant to appraise. If she wasn't so preoccupied by her own problems, she suspected those blue eyes of his could be quite devastating. Judging by the dozen or so women hanging on his every word and movement here in the hall, Sarah would have a long line in front of her.

Not that she'd ever get in such a line in the first place. He'd put her in the *back* of a wagon, taken her to the ranch in a purposely bone-jarring manner, and been completely unfazed and unapologetic about her torn dress. Despite his appealing looks, he was easy to be angry with. Odd, however, that she had the feeling she'd been mad at him...before all this.

Regardless, Sarah did not appreciate his sense of humor or his vindictiveness. She did wonder what she'd done to offend the man. Or if he'd simply taken a dislike to her for no reason.

April slid over, grinning ear to ear. "Nice to look at, isn't he?"

"I beg your pardon?"

"Nick. He's a far cry from ugly. But you'd have to get in line. There's several pairs of eyes fluttering at him, *yah*? Even though it is against the rules."

Sarah withdrew to stir the remaining bits of food on her plate. "Rules?"

"The men are ordered to leave us alone, but, oh, that Hub." April rolled her eyes and pulled away. "He flirts the way men breathe. It just comes natural to him."

"I don't believe I've met him. Why the rule, do you think? About the no fraternizing with us? The ladies." She looked up again and studied the room. Thinning out now. But a few women remained. Some of them hid their wounds well. Some didn't. Were they abused? Drunks? Abandoned? What could bring so many women to this ranch? Who was Miss Sally?

"You've probably figured out we're all here because we need to—."

"Get a second chance. Yes, Miss Sally said something about it."

"Well, some of us are getting over some very bad heartbreaks. We are"—she rolled her fingers around in the air, as if the action would make the right word leap to her mind—"vulnerable. The men have strict orders to keep their distance."

Mr. Bannister nodded in agreement with Miss Sally and strode down the center of the hall to the exit, his movements tracked by most of the women in the room. Wounded, maybe, but these ladies were not blind. On the other hand, the head cowboy seemed oblivious to the attention he garnered.

April tracked her gaze. "He plays by the rules. He is never anything but a perfect gentleman." Sarah scowled at April, whose eyes widened at the look. "What'd I say?"

"He's not the gentleman you think he is."

"Really? Did he flirt with you?"

"No. Quite the opposite. He seems to dislike me."

"Nick? You must be confused. He likes everybody."

Sarah once again relived the jarring ride from town and the aloof, unconcerned cowboy driving the wagon. "Everybody but me."

And the feeling was mutual.

SARAH STARED out the window at the ranch washed in silvery moonlight and haunting shadows, and released a sigh. Behind her, the soft breaths and gentle snores of dozens of women filled the dormitory. Her new roommates. She wondered about her old ones.

Family? Parents? Or a husband? Did she have children out there somewhere missing her?

"You get used to it."

A soft voice startled her, and she turned as Melissa Evans joined her at the window. They'd chatted briefly on the way back from dinner. So many new faces, it was a wonder Sarah remembered her name.

"Used to what?" she whispered.

"The snoring. The open room. The lack of privacy."

"Oh. Yes, I suppose I will. To be truthful, I hadn't given it much thought."

The girl nodded. She was pretty, with long, startlingly black hair, big brown eyes, and skin that held a hint of something exotic. Perhaps Spanish. "April said you don't remember who you are. Is that true?"

"Yes."

She tsked. "Wish I could have been that lucky. Lots of things in my past I'd like to forget."

"You say that, but trust me, it's unnerving. I feel like I'm standing on the edge of a big, black hole. My life is in it somewhere, but I can't fish it out."

Melissa nodded sympathetically. "I guess that would be awful. Forgetting family. Friends. If they're people you want to remember."

She faded off at the end, and Sarah understood. Like everyone she'd met here so far, there was something lurking in all their pasts.

"On Thursday nights," the girl said, changing the subject, "we all gather in the parlor. Miss Sally does a Bible study. It's good. You should come. Anybody can get your memory back, it's God."

Sarah couldn't argue with that. But it made her wonder, had she left a relationship with the Lord somewhere in that black hole, too?

"Well, I'm getting a little chilled." Melissa rubbed her

arms. “Don’t stay up too late. We get up at the crack of dawn around here.”

“All right. Thank you.” After a minute, Sarah slipped into her own little cot and stared up at the bunk above her. The darkness around her pressed in. She didn’t want to shut her eyes and see more of it.

Anybody can get your memory back, it’s God.

The words stuck in her head. *I don’t know if I know You, God, but if You’re there, I could use the help...*

CHAPTER SIX

With a primal growl, Kevin lobbed his empty sherry glass across his office. It shattered with an almost gentle sound. Not the effect he'd hoped for. His detective, the sharply-dressed, silver-haired Mr. William Devonshire, moved his head coolly to the side as it flew by, but didn't cower. No, not Mr. Devonshire.

"I'm sorry the news upsets you," he said with a distinguished air, "but we're, of course, still looking."

"The woman simply didn't fall off the face of the planet!" Kevin bellowed, pushing his wavy, blond hair back off his forehead. "One minute she's in a train station and the next she's gone." He jabbed his finger down on his desk. "I'm paying you to find her. Do it!"

"We're checking—"

"I don't think you understand what hangs in the balance." Enraged by the detective's calm demeanor, Kevin pinched his brow to refrain from throwing an ashtray at him. "My political future," he said slowly, in case the famed detective had trouble following. "Her father has married royalty. He's the most well-connected man in Colorado now. I have my sights on Washington. He supports my plans…but not without his daughter on my arm."

"Mr. Hartman, I'm well aware of your ambitions." Devonshire didn't exactly glare at Kevin, but his gaze was intense and cold. "We're checking all the train stops in a hundred-mile radius. We're doing our best to find and question passengers who should have been on the platform that morning. Some of *your* associates concern me, however."

"My associates?"

"Miss Caldwell's father says the girl is headstrong and stubborn. And that she has no desire to marry you. Her absence could be of her own making. However, I'm aware of some of your dealings with the Clanton and Murphy families. Dangerous groups, both of them."

"You're suggesting they've taken Sierra?" Kevin frowned. He believed he was on good terms with both groups. He'd laundered quite a bit of ill-gotten gains for them, especially recently. The transactions had gone smoothly. He shook his head. "There are no candidates for sainthood among them, but currently, I believe they are satisfied with my services."

"You've received no ransom notes from them or anyone else?"

Kevin was offended by the bald insinuation. "Your question implies I could be holding back such information."

"Are you?"

"How dare you?" Kevin's temper got the better of him. He grabbed the ashtray and threw it at Mr. Devonshire with wicked force. The man dodged it easily again, pivoting sideways with the grace of a dancer, and the projectile flew past him, crashing into the wall, shattering loudly. Kevin wished he'd thrown it first. "You work for me. You are clear on that, aren't you?"

Devonshire cut his eyes at Kevin. "You should get a handle on your temper, sir. Outbursts like that can get a man in trouble. Especially one with ambition."

"What are you saying?"

"That you never answered my question."

Was the man trying to get Kevin to throw his letter opener at him next? His fingers crawled toward the bone-handled blade, even as he attempted to squash his fury over the impertinence. "I need her back. I don't know where she is. I don't believe anyone I know is involved with her disappearance. I want you to find her." He raised his eyebrows, asking without words if the detective was satisfied.

The gentleman nodded. "I'll be in touch."

After a physical examination, the doctor asked Sarah to dress and meet him and Miss Sally downstairs in the office. Sarah agreed, with a slight huff. She could have told them that no backwoods, Hickville ranch doctor could solve the problem. She needed to have her head examined by a real professional. A doctor from Chicago or New York.

At the same time, however, she didn't want to deal with the medical establishment. She buttoned the last fob on her shirtwaist, smoothed out the wrinkles in her split skirt, and headed to Miss Sally's office.

Doc Hanson, a grizzled old man with a bushy beard and a good seventy or so years under his belt, was muttering in low tones as Sarah entered. She did not appreciate that, either. "If you're discussing my health"—

she shut the large, oak door behind her—"don't you think it's rude to whisper?"

He tugged on his ear and nodded. "Mebbe so. Didn't think the whole ranch needed to hear it, though."

A bit chastised, Sarah flicked a glance at Miss Sally and then took a seat. "Your prognosis, doctor. I assume you must have some thoughts on my condition."

He frowned slightly at her tone. "Well, miss, you don't seem to have any obvious physical trauma. You've got a few bruises, almost like you fell, and maybe you had a slight concussion. That's my guess."

"Enough of a concussion to cause amnesia?"

"Lots of things can do that. Doesn't always have to be a physical trauma."

"If not physical, what? Disease?"

"You said you're not having any headaches."

"No, other than the one I awoke with on the train."

He made a tsk sound and folded his arms. "You can't remember anything? Anything at all about your past?"

She sighed. He'd asked her this question repeatedly. "Nothing. I told you. Blank slate."

That seemed to intrigue Miss Sally, who raised her chin and looked at Dr. Hanson. "You said it doesn't always have to be physical. What then? Mental? You think she's chosen to forget?"

"I beg your pardon," Sarah objected. "You make me sound as if I'm insane."

"No, no." The old doctor patted the air. "She just means you could be running from something."

"Something traumatic?" The idea appalled Sarah. How very…melodramatic.

"Doesn't always have to be traumatic. Between the bump on your head and whatever your circumstances are—or were—maybe forgetting is by choice. Subconsciously."

Sarah's mouth fell open. The doctor was implying this was all her fault. He read her face. "Miss, the brain is a complex, mysterious organ. We don't understand it. I don't think we ever will. My advice is, if you want to get to the bottom of this, and make sure you're not carrying around a tumor in that head of yours, see a specialist."

"A tumor?" This actually frightened Sarah.

"I don't buy into the idea. At least, not right now. If you start getting headaches, blurred vision, dizziness, then I'd say the specialist becomes mandatory."

Sarah wilted a little in the chair. She did not care for anything the doctor had said. "What if I'm not sick? And what if I do want to remember?"

"Then time might be your answer. You settle down, relax a little, get comfortable with your environment, all those memories might come rushing back in like a flood."

"A flood." To remember everything in the blink of an eye. What would it all reveal? Did she want to know? *Was* she running from something?

Or someone?

"There is one last idea."

Sarah looked up, intrigued by the hesitancy in the doctor's voice. Out of the corner of her eye, she could see Miss Sally watching.

He shoved his hands into his pockets and rocked on his heels. "You could be making this up."

"What?" Sarah surged to her feet. "How dare you call me a liar."

"I did no such thing. I just questioned your version of what's going on."

For some reason, she looked to Miss Sally, strangely

eager for the woman to believe her. "I am not lying. I cannot remember anything before the train. I wish I could. I feel lost, like a blank page."

Miss Sally's gaze was intense, penetrating. After a moment, she nodded. "We've got her, Doc. We'll take care of her. And we'll see about the specialist, if necessary."

NICK AND HUB whooped and hollered and pushed a small group of nursing cows and calves into the wash with the rest of the herd. From across the draw, one of the girls waved her hat, acknowledging that the animals had been added. Nick waved back and then spun his horse back around.

"Come on, Hub, I've got something I want to do before we head back."

"Ah, not that again."

Nick ignored the whiny complaint and spurred his horse. He and Hub rode for about half an hour till they topped the rim of a low, pine-studded mesa. Here, Nick pulled up on the reins and drank in the view. A pretty valley, green as any in Ireland, rolled and dipped in a long oblong shape back up to the mountains. A small but swift creek crossed it almost exactly in the center. Near the bank, a ramshackle, dilapidated cabin with a sagging roof sat alone and forlorn.

His old home place.

He trotted down the hill and pulled up at the hitching post. Hub reined in beside him. "Sheesh. If this was mine, I'd level it and start over."

"It's not yours," Nick reminded him curtly. "I grew up here. Got a lot of good memories."

"I can't believe you're still dreaming about this place. It's a money hole."

"It's anything but. And I'll make it pay. One day, I'll turn it into a fine, respectable ranch. Maybe no Burning Dress or Bar T but it'll provide."

"I think you're whistling Dixie."

"It's got plenty of water and good, rich grass. Nothing wrong with this spread." He slid out of the saddle and stepped cautiously up to the front door. The front porch was still stout and did not seem to be deteriorating. He pushed the door open, again surprised it still swung freely, and let himself into the two-room cabin. Cobwebs, dirt, and debris covered the floor and kitchen cabinets, and a broken rocking chair sat catty-wompass by the fireplace.

He righted the chair and tried to imagine the place all cleaned up and painted like it had been. A pretty little wife in a clean, white apron, cooking dinner on the stove. Two kids, little fellas, playing marbles in front of the fireplace. Yeah, one day this place was going to be his home again.

"Just about got the mortgage paid off, and the taxes are current. I need to do something with it."

"How 'bout sell it?" Hub suggested from the doorway, his thumbs hooked lazily in his back pockets.

"Nah." Nick rested his hand on the hearth and let the rush of memories roll over him. His momma's roast and potatoes—the best ever. Served on a pretty, round oak table that had long since been sold. And they used to put the Christmas tree in that far corner. He remembered his first gun, a .22, propped up against the wall and wrapped in brown paper and red ribbons.

Then the hard times had come. Blizzards. Droughts. Disease. Death. The life of a rancher.

He snatched himself back to the moment and glanced at Hub. "I'll bring this place back to life. And it'll be a good home."

A ROOSTER CROWED as Nick stepped out of the bunkhouse. He stretched with a yawn and slapped his hat on. The sun was just peeking over the distant mountains, and the sky was aglow with a pretty mix of oranges and blues. One day, he'd have a view like this from his own front porch.

He just had to be patient. Keep saving up his money.

"Nick, good morning."

He turned at Miss Sally's voice and nodded a greeting as he stepped off the porch toward her. She strode across the yard, a tall, slender figure in britches, but she didn't wear them like she was trying to prove a point. She just had chores to do. She worked hard and expected the same from her hands, and Nick was all right with that.

Sleepy chickens skittered out of her way as she reached him and offered a morning shake with one hand, and held a steaming cup of coffee in the other. "Fresh coffee in the main kitchen."

"Punchie made some. I had a cup. What can I do for you?"

Almost as tall as he was, she rested a hand on his shoulder and nudged him to walk with her. Not resisting, he let her lead him. They headed toward the barn as she spoke. "I need a favor, Nick. I've got some business to tend to in town this morning. I'd like you to get Sarah started on some minor chores."

His steps faltered, then he stopped altogether. "Um, I don't mean any disrespect, ma'am, but nursemaid isn't part of my job." She quirked an eyebrow at him, and the authority behind it had him backing up. He tugged on his shirt and cleared his throat. "I guess, on the other hand, I should consider that you have a reason for asking."

"That would be wise of you, since I don't make a habit of assigning my hands fool's errands."

They started walking again and she sighed. "I want to get you a little more involved in helping manage the ranch. What do you say to that?"

"Any reason for the change? You hired me as a cowboy."

"I know you bought your pa's ranch back and you want to get it up and running again. I want to help you."

"It's going to take a while."

"Good things usually do. Anything worth having is worth waiting for. In the meantime, there is a lot you can learn helping run Burning Dress."

He nodded, stopped walking again. "This some kind of promotion?"

"In pay, yes. But some of the things I want you to do may seem beneath you."

"Like getting Sarah on task?"

"That's where I want you to start. Then come see me later. I've got some production numbers I want to go over with you."

Miss Sally started to walk away, but Nick was still confused. "Wait, well, I mean, guess I should say thank you first."

"You're welcome, but I'm sure you'll make a fine assistant foreman. I'll be thanking you soon, I bet."

"Well, uh, what do you think I should do first with Sarah?"

A wry smile lifted the corner of the woman's mouth. "Figure it out. That's what I'm paying you for."

It didn't occur to him until she'd walked away that he'd never asked about his new pay rate.

Regardless, he had to figure out this little test the boss lady had tossed him. What in the world did an assistant foreman do with a hand who, as far as everybody was concerned, had an unknown amount of experience on a ranch?

As far as everybody was concerned?

What was he thinking? He needed to come clean and tell Miss Sally and Sarah—er, Sierra—what he knew. It would be easier now, before the water got too deep. Just tell them it dawned on him where he knew her from.

He just about had himself convinced when Sarah stepped out the back door. She had her hair pulled back out of the way but tucked an escaped strand behind her ear. Sighing, she smoothed down her skirt and was tugging on her gloves when she spotted him watching her. That haughty chin of hers came up and she strode toward him.

Dang if that arrogant attitude of hers didn't just fly all over him.

One day. He'd take one day to show her what life was like for a regular, hard-working ranch hand. Then he'd 'fess up.

"Good morning. I understand you'll be assigning me some work today."

She sounded inconvenienced, as if her champagne wasn't properly chilled. Oh, how she rubbed him the wrong way, like sandpaper against the grain, but he hid it with a smile and motioned toward the barn.

"On a ranch," he began, and they started walking, "especially one this size, there are a lot of different crews you can fall in with. Miss Sally has a kitchen garden, but she's also a commercial farmer. We're growing wheat, corn, and alfalfa. That's one crew. She's got another that does maintenance around the ranch, fixing, painting, and building. Then there's everything that comes along with running a ranch."

"Like the cowboy work," she said, her tone mocking. "Ropin' and ridin'—"

"There's more to it than just sitting in the saddle moving cattle around. Range management keeps the herd healthy but doesn't allow over-grazing. We've also got to keep the fences maintained—miles of them. We have to manage the herd so we can keep a count of heifers and calves. There's the work involved in calculating feed and yields, and keeping an eye on all the animals for sickness and disease. To name some of the work. And there's a whole other crew that manages the remuda."

Her expression softened a touch. "What's a remuda?"

"The horses for the ranch."

"Oh."

He watched her for any sign the idea of horses might appeal to her, but her gaze was on the ranch around them, coming to life in the early morning light. And he figured this was as good a place as any to start. An idea struck him then, courtesy of his mischievous brother and a certain event from his own past about a dozen years earlier.

"Um, well"—he slapped his thighs—"since you're still recovering from a bump on the head, let's keep you close to the ranch for a few days."

"I'm not an invalid."

"Maybe you're not. Maybe you are. So, we'll keep it simple. Milk the cows and gather the eggs from the henhouse." He knew Gilly normally did this, but he'd find her and let her know. Second in charge of the kitchen, she often passed these chores off to new guests.

Sarah's lips tightened a little, a pinch appeared on her forehead. "Cows. Chickens." She shook her head. "They don't ring any bells, that's for sure."

"Maybe they will. Come on."

He led the way into the barn. In the two back stalls on the right, fussy Guernsey cows moaned their displeasure at being ignored. Nick dropped his hand on the stall door. "Anything coming back to you?"

She peered into the stall, eyed the milk stool and the high, bony rear end of the animal with obvious skepticism. The poor girl's udder was ready for milking. Sarah gulped. "Not a thing."

He started to prompt her to go ahead in, but that saucy little chin came up and she entered on her own. Nick admitted a little grudging admiration.

The cow was affable and eager for the expected milking. She didn't sense, or at least care, that the human in the stall was moving like she might need to bolt at any second. Keeping her back to the stall wall, and arm's length from the Guernsey, Sarah lifted the milking stool off a wall hook and held it in front of her. Then she looked at the cow as if she wasn't sure at which end to start.

Nick bit his lip to hide a smile and pointed at the udder. "You start there."

"I know that," she snapped. "I'm not incompetent. I just don't recall—*nothing* about this feels familiar. At all."

Gritting her teeth, she inched toward the cow and set down the stool, her head pulled back as if the animal might be dangerous. Then she eased onto the seat. She wiggled her fingers for a moment, then slowly moved them toward the udder.

She looks like she's about to diffuse a Confederate landmine. "You want some pointers?"

She paused and tossed him a scowl. "I do not." She frowned at the swollen udder. "How hard can this be?"

Her brows knit and lips tensed, she reached out and gingerly grasped a teat. The Guernsey bleated in surprise and launched a high kick. Sarah squealed as she dodged the leg and fell over backward into the hay, from where she immediately scrambled to her feet. Moving like the cow might be on the attack, she flew to the corner, her hands raised for protection. Or maybe in surrender.

"What's the matter with her? Why did she do that? Is she dangerous?"

Nick had to look away and get the laughter under control and out of his voice. "I guess I should have warned you about cold hands."

Her green eyes sparkled at him, and he was sure at that moment that daggers were going to come flying out of them. "You *guess* you should have warned me?"

He shrugged, enjoying this entirely too much. "I did offer."

"Vat ees going on here?"

Nick looked over as Gilly joined them. A rotund, thick woman with bright red cheeks, she was a German farm girl who had probably milked a thousand cows.

"Miss Sally asked me to put the new girl here on— Oh, Sarah—Gilly." He motioned back and forth between them. "Gilly—Sarah. Sarah here on some simple chores," he continued. "Turns out she needs some pointers."

"Yes, Mees Sally tell me you were out here with her. And about the chores. I vill help her. She vill do the chickens also?"

"I thought so."

"Ya, that's good. She vill tend to the sheep and goats as vell."

Nick slapped the stall fence. "Sounds like a plan."

"Miss Sally said see her after lunch."

"All right. I'll check back with you two later." He nodded at Sarah, paused over the heat coming off her expression, and had to clamp his jaw down to keep from grinning. She was madder than a wet hen caught in a spring rain.

"Thank you, Mr. Bannister." The edge in her tone could have cut a steak. "I'm glad my difficulties provide you such amusement."

He let the grin break. "What doesn't kill you makes you stronger, Princess."

"Then I hope I survive your management skills."

Gilly's eyes widened over all the sharp banter. "I think you go now." She gave Nick a good shove. "Ve take care of the milk."

He walked off chuckling. True, his entertainment had been at her expense. It was a small thing, though, considering the way she'd talked to him in Denver. But he wouldn't let this get out of hand. "Just a little fun, Lord," he whispered. "Then I'll confess."

WHAT DOESN'T KILL you makes you stronger.

Sarah glared at Nick Bannister's back as he jauntily sauntered off. She wondered if stringing him up from the hayloft by his feet would make *him* stronger.

"Now, you don't mind him," Gilly said, entering the stall. "Stick your hands into your armpits and watch me."

"I beg your pardon?"

Gilly righted the stool, then stood and folded her arms across her sizable chest, barely managing to shove her hands into her armpits. "For varmth. Like this."

"I see." Sarah followed the order.

"Now, come here and vatch."

Sarah obeyed, moving carefully up to Gilly's side, while keeping a close eye out for another flying hoof. The woman rubbed her hands together for a few seconds and then grabbed a teat. While she gripped it, she appeared to simultaneously tug downward on it. "You must have a firm grip and pull down vith pressure, but not too hard."

Sarah leaned in and started a little at the spurt of milk that hit the bucket. Gilly leaned into the animal, pressing her ruddy cheek against the stomach, and worked her hands rhythmically for a few minutes. "See, eet's not so hard, yes?"

"You make it look easy." And maybe it was, with a little practice, but getting within kicking distance of the cow's hoof held no appeal for Sarah.

"Good. Then you try." Gilly rose and motioned for Sarah to take the stool.

Sarah wanted to argue. In fact, she wanted to scream at this large, capable woman. She wanted to scream at the cow. And she wanted to scream at heaven above for this situation. Everything about this felt unfamiliar, alien, and downright wrong. Yet, the name Burning Dress Ranch had been burned into her mind.

Perplexed, she gulped and sat down.

This time, when she touched the teat, the cow did not react. Encouraged, Sarah made a few awkward tugs. With no results.

"Like this," Gilly said patiently. "I show you." She put her hands over Sarah's, tightened her grip, and repeated her actions from before. Sarah studied the feel of the motion, the rhythm to it. As more milk spurted into the pail, Gilly stepped back, smiling. Now Sarah was smiling. She was doing it. She was milking a cow.

"Keep that up. I return vith another pail."

Sarah started to blurt out *don't leave me* but she didn't want to wreck the work she was accomplishing. So, instead, she placed her cheek against the cow's stomach and kept up the task.

"You must be the new gal."

"She is, and she is busy," Gilly said firmly.

Sarah glanced up, momentarily taken aback by the handsome cowboy grinning at her. He was a striking man with mischievous humor dancing in his brown eyes, and the broad, toothy smile was both inviting and vexing. Sarah shook off his spell and focused on the task in her hands.

"Aw, Gilly, you know I came in here to see you. See if I could sneak a kiss."

Gilly gasped and pushed the cowboy back. "You have no shame, Hub. No shame. Get out." She began pushing the resistant cowboy. "Get out and don't bother us."

"Not even one kiss?" he said, trying to lean into her, while stealing glances at Sarah.

"You go," Gilly demanded, "before I turn you over my knee."

Hub backed off and winked over his shoulder. "You promise?"

Gilly blushed down into her neckline. Scowling, but clearly not angry, she grabbed the troublemaker by his collar and the seat of his pants and helped him on his way.

Over the top of the stall, Sarah could see him laughing silently as he skittered out of the woman's grip.

"I'll be back," he said, spinning around and backing away from her. He tipped his hat at both women and jogged out of the barn.

Gilly returned to the stall, wiping her hands as if she'd just handled a challenging task and had won easily. Sarah wasn't so sure.

"Who was that?" she asked conversationally, really pumping out the milk now.

"His name is Hub. He is like a glass doll. Very pretty on the outside. Nothing on the inside."

"You don't like him?"

"Oh, I like him very much. Who could help it? He is very funny. But I vould never fall in love vith him. The girls who do, he just breaks their hearts. You keep that in mind, yes?"

The advice puzzled Sarah. "Oh, absolutely." The last thing she wanted was a man in her life right now, but if Hub had a long list of broken hearts, it was probably advice given to all the new girls. After all, he was more vivacious than the reserved Mr. Bannister.

"He seems more friendly than your other hand."

"Nick? Oh, Nick is a good man. Solid, steady, honest. The girl who gets him vill vin a real prize." Gilly frowned, the expression seeming uncharacteristic on her face. "He usually gets along vith everyone."

Sarah heard the question in the woman's voice. Instead of explaining, she looked at the pail. Nearly full. And she'd done most of the work herself. She was pleased at having learned a new skill.

At least, it felt like a new skill.

"I let Hub get away vith too much," Gilly said, drawing circles on the stall's top rail with her index finger. "He is not supposed to flirt with any of us. It is against the rules, but he makes us laugh."

Sarah could see the man's appeal.

The bucket was closing in on filling up and she stopped her work. "I guess you'd better hand me that bucket."

She carefully lifted the pail, which was heavier than she'd expected, and took a step back. As she turned to Gilly and lifted her foot to move around the stool, the cow shifted, bumping into her. Off balance, she stepped forward but caught the edge of the stool. It tipped over beneath her boot.

"Oh," she wailed as she bumped into the cow again, sloshing half the milk down the front of her outfit.

"Oh, careful," Gilly yelled, reaching out.

Somehow, Sarah's feet tangled in the upended stool and she tripped headlong…

Spilling the rest of the fresh milk into the hay at Gilly's feet. Sarah dropped her head, sick over the accident. "Oh, I can't believe I did that." She felt a tap on her head and looked up.

Gilly was holding the empty pail out to her. "Make sure Dolly is done and then ve vill do Mabelle."

Sarah climbed to her feet and took the bucket. "I'm sorry."

Gilly eyed the wet hay at her feet and winced. "Is not good, but you vill be more careful now."

Sarah appreciated the woman's patience. With a nod, she turned back to Dolly.

SALLY CLOSED her eyes and took a moment to listen. And feel. A gentle summer breeze lifted a few fine strands of silver hair and tickled her cheek, which she raised toward the sun. The warmth felt nice, and she let it seep into her soul. The horse shifted beneath her, the saddle squeaking with the movement. The animal blew, puttering his lips, not impatient but ready for a run.

Around her, the long, gently sloping valley was silent, except for the occasional sound of the wind coming down from the tops of some nearby lodgepole pines. There were a million places in the universe to be alone, but she doubted anywhere was as peaceful as this little valley.

"Good morning." Sam Hain, in his precise English drawl, called to her from the shadows of the trees. "Imagine meeting you here."

Sally frowned and opened her eyes. Sam nudged his horse, and the animal ambled toward her. She'd never get over what a dapper figure he painted, always wearing a fine suit and kid-leather riding gloves. He sat in the saddle with ramrod posture, commanding and confident. Wavy black hair peeked out beneath his hat, which hid his face in shadow, but she knew he was smiling. He was always smiling when he found her out here.

He rode up and tipped his Stetson, then tilted that handsome face toward her. In his fifties, he could easily pass for much younger. A coal black beard and mustache streaked fashionably with a little gray traced a mouth that still dared her to kiss it. His dark eyes, however, were where her calm wavered. They never failed to make her heart speed up a notch. They glimmered with mischief. Would the butterflies never go away?

"Good to see you, Sally."

Simple words, yet everything Sam said had double meanings. "You too," she said flatly.

"Mind if I ride along with you?"

She toyed with the idea of objecting. "I came out here to pray."

His mouth twitched up in the corner. "I know."

Devil, she thought. And she was as vulnerable as ever to his dangerous charms. No, she corrected herself. She could be charmed by him. She'd never be fooled again. She signaled her mare and the animal struck out at a lazy pace. Sam fell in beside her.

"Any new or interesting guests out at Burning Dress?"

Immediately, she thought of Sarah. "A young lady came in a few days ago. Strange case. She's got amnesia."

"Amnesia?" He ran his tongue over his teeth. "That is interesting, certainly. I'm sure you're aware of her past?"

"No."

He drew his horse to a stop. "No?"

She did not oblige his shock or curiosity by also stopping, merely kept her horse at the same pace. After a moment, he rejoined her.

"That's unusual, isn't it? Don't you always get—?"

"At least an inkling? Yes. Not this time."

"Why, do you suppose?"

She flicked a glance heavenward. *Exactly, Father. Why?* "Maybe He just wants me to practice a little more trust."

"The way you so blindly accept everything He sends you, I would think trust isn't something you need to work on."

In his own, caustic way, Sam had paid her a compliment. "Then it's information I don't need yet," she said.

He sighed. "Ours is not to reason why?"

"You're mocking me. Did you come out here to pick a fight?"

Out of the corner of her eye, she saw him sag a little. "No, I did not. My apologies."

"You're forgiven." He tensed instantly and she flinched at the unintended pun. "You could be, you know," she said, trying to salvage the conversation before it fell off a cliff. "Never too late to turn the ship around. Ever since you killed Chauncey you've gone—" She didn't dare speak it aloud. A ranch hand from another ranch had taken a shot at Sally. Sam had dealt harshly and swiftly with the man, and the action had seemed to accelerate a dark, downward spiral in her old friend.

"Say it. Darker," he whispered, staring off into the distance. "I've gone more toward the darkness again."

"Yes." Sally's heart ached for this man, who had been caught in some awful tug of war his whole life. "Like you were in the old days…almost. I don't see you with a girl's eyes now, though. I'm wiser."

He looked down and drummed his fingers on his pommel. "And I'm not so dashing anymore?"

"I romanticized you back then." She nudged her horse closer and let her leg touch his. He almost jerked away, as if she'd sparked a bolt of static, but their eyes locked and he froze. "I see you for what you are, Sam, but I also see what you can become. I'll never give up praying for that."

He snorted in disgust and backed his roan away. "An exercise in futility."

"You know He's God of the impossible." When he didn't reply, she circled back to the reason for his interruption. "Why did you come out here today?"

He took a long time to answer. "No reason. No reason at all."

He moved to spur his horse, but she stopped him with an extended arm. "It was wrong, but killing Chauncey showed me something about you."

"And what is that?"

"You didn't murder him. You said you gave him a

chance. But you went after him because of me. It was selfless of you."

"I beg to differ. It was vengeance, and I was never in any danger."

"Yes, but you did what you did to avenge someone other than yourself."

He scratched his chin. "Aren't you the one always telling me vengeance is not mine to hand out?"

"You're missing my point."

"Apparently. Please explain it."

She grimaced at his tone and shook her head. "There was another person in the equation besides yourself. That gives me hope."

"Do you never tire of looking for the silver lining?"

She laughed, recalling how many times he'd chided her for the dauntless hope. "No."

Her answer and her direct stare seemed to throw him off. No small feat. He cleared his throat and picked up the reins again. "I'll leave you to your prayer time. Tell Him I said hello."

CHAPTER SEVEN

WITH THE SPLASH OF FRESH MILK STIFFENING HER clothing, Sarah did indeed endeavor to be more careful with all her chores that day. Yet, none of them came easily. Gilly guided her around the hen house, a large affair housing two dozen chickens in a big, warm shed. Gilly demonstrated how to reach in and steal eggs. Like milking a cow, deceptively easy.

When Sarah tried, the chicken pecked her hand, drawing blood. Gilly chuckled. "I get you some gloves tomorrow." Then, as if her skin was made of iron, she reached in quickly, lifted the hen up, and snatched the egg before the bird had a chance to protest again.

From this moment on, Sarah was gun-shy of every chicken, yet most of them were not apt to peck. But the ones who did set her confidence back every time. Finally, the wire basket full, she followed Gilly to the next chore, vengefully hoping for chicken for dinner.

Next came the goats. A small corral of half an acre or so housed about eight goats, all of different sizes, shapes, and colors. At Sarah and Gilly's approach, all the heads swung up in their direction. Bleating and crying erupted from the group, eager to be fed, and the critters swarmed them.

"Spread out the food for them." Gilly pointed at the long, wooden trough. Sarah began pouring the food out, walking along the side of it. She noticed out of the corner of her eye that Gilly was looking around the area, a pensive dip in her brow.

The trough full, Sarah turned and was striding back toward Gilly when something crashed into her rear end. Taken completely by surprise, her knees buckled, and she went down, her right hand landing perfectly in a fresh pile of excrement.

Gilly rushed past her, waving her arms. "Back, you little demon! Back."

Cringing at what was on her hand, Sarah scrambled to her feet and spun. Gilly was gesticulating wildly at a Billy goat, who was in fast retreat. "That little devil," Sarah muttered.

"You stay back," Gilly yelled again at the goat and began walking backward. She motioned at Sarah to follow her lead, and in the next moment, the woman was locking the gate behind them. Sarah wiped her hand off on the bottom rail of the fence, her face actually aching from the grimace stuck there.

"He is feeling randy today. Keep an eye on him ven you feed."

The fence not removing all the excrement, Sarah wiped her hand through a thick patch of grass. When she stood up, Gilly handed her a handkerchief. She wiped her hand and sighed. None of these chores or these animals was jogging anything loose in her brain. She would be shocked if her past did include farm life. "Next?"

"Blue, the hog."

FEEDING the hog turned out to be the easiest chore. Gilly handed her a bucket of slop and pointed at the trough. "Climb up there and pour it in over the fence. Never go in with the hog."

Sarah took the pail and wrinkled her nose at the mess in it. Then she slid her gaze over the fence to the fat, brown swine lying in the mud a few feet away. At her approach, he snorted and rose to his feet with surprising agility. Sarah was taken aback by the animal's girth. "My, he's a big boy."

"And he can be mean. You be careful." She pointed at a stool next to the fence. "No tripping."

Sarah climbed up, dumped the bucket, and the hog grunted his approval as he dove his snout into the grotesque, rotting food.

"Well, ladies, how is it going?"

Sarah turned at Mr. Bannister's voice. He took his hat off, and then his brow arched sky high as he appraised her. A little unnerved, Sarah looked down at her clothes. The milk, yellowing and beginning to smell, stained the front of her shirtwaist and split skirt. Smudges of dirt marred the area over her stomach where she'd incessantly wiped her hands. Her knees were black with mud stains from falling in the goat pen. Self-consciously, she plucked a piece of straw from her hair.

"It's going just fine," she said, raising her chin.

Gilly shrugged. "She's not the vorst hand I've ever had."

Mr. Bannister passed a black-gloved hand over his

mouth, clearly hiding yet another smile. She wondered why he bothered with the motion.

"You look like you've had a tussle or two, Duchess," he said.

Again, with the royal titles. Oh, how they annoyed her. "A few trip-ups. Nothing that will happen again."

"Anything coming back to you?"

Sarah puzzled over his expression. He was amused by something, but also…troubled. Could he actually be concerned for her well-being? "No. Nothing familiar or compelling about working with farm animals. Especially chickens."

"We'll give it some time. In the meantime, there's always places to pitch-in on a ranch."

"If you say so."

Miss Sally's house was large and comfortable, the size of a small hotel. After dinner, Sarah walked the hallway that led from the front door to the large, stone-covered patio out back. She thought she might watch the fireflies. A warm, summer evening had to entice them out.

She stepped outside in the fading light and breathed in the scent of fresh-cut hay. Crickets and frogs sang in a symphony presented down at the pond. She rubbed her arms against the slight mountain chill and strode over to the edge of the stone paving. Movement caught her eye, and she realized Miss Sally was relaxing in the log swing several yards away. Around her, lightning bugs flitted and blinked their presence.

As Sarah watched, dozens of the bugs gathered in the vicinity of the woman, as if she were some kind of beacon. Almost like candles on a tree, they illuminated a small area around her, dipping and floating and blinking. Then, most amazing of all, Miss Sally lifted her hand and waved it back and forth as if she were conducting an orchestra, and the bugs responded.

Sarah blinked. In *unison,* the insects moved to the left, to the right, up, or down depending on where Miss Sally's hand went. Then Sarah noticed the frogs and crickets, how their volume seemed to coincide with her hand movements as well, going louder, softer, longer, shorter.

Sarah couldn't understand what she was seeing or hearing. Then Miss Sally laughed, clapped her hands, and said loudly, "Well, praise the Lord. Thank you. Thank you!"

As if dismissed, the lightning bugs disbanded, flying all over the manicured lawn behind the house, and the crickets and frogs found their own, discordant rhythm. Sarah frowned. This made no sense. How could a woman—?

Miss Sally rose and came toward her. "Beautiful evening, isn't it?"

"Yes. Yes. Um..." Sarah tripped over her tongue. She couldn't think. She wanted to ask what she'd just seen, but her mouth and brain wouldn't work together.

"I'm headed to bed. Enjoy the lightning bugs. They're in rare form tonight."

Sarah felt incapable of forming a question. "Yes. Yes. I will. Thank you."

She stayed outside for a while watching the random, blinking lights attached to the little icons of summer. By the time she was ready for bed, she'd convinced herself she'd only imagined nature's strange behavior around Miss Sally.

CHAPTER EIGHT

"NICK, THANK YOU FOR JOINING US."

He quietly shut the door to Miss Sally's office behind him and strode up to her desk. "Sure thing."

Lowdy, the Burning Dress's foreman, sat in a chair in front of her desk. He tagged Nick friendly-like on the leg. "Mornin', boy."

"Mornin'." Lowdy was only forty but had the whitest hair Nick had ever seen on anybody under seventy. He was spry, too. Full of energy, and had a good head for ranching. Nick had learned quite a bit from him already and expected to keep it up.

Miss Sally leaned back in her chair and waved a letter at them. She was interrupted as she was about to speak by her cat, Little Joe. A furry, smoky-gray critter of impressive proportions, he leaped imperially onto her desk. Eyeing the two men with obvious disapproval, the cat strutted over and sat down in front of his owner.

Miss Sally huffed impatiently at the cat. "What have I told you about interrupting me when I have company?"

Just as dismissively, Miss Sally waved the cat away. "Go to the kitchen and have some cream."

As if understanding every word of the command, the cat turned, jumped to the floor, and strode out the back way, apparently headed to the kitchen. Nick's jaw must have been hanging open at the spectacle. Lowdy chuckled. "You get used to it. All the animals listen to her like that."

"As well they should," Miss Sally said, once more waving the letter. "Nick, I have to make some banking decisions. Considering everything your father went through with First Colorado and Jason Caldwell, I thought you might like to know about the changes around here. A good relationship with a bank is—"

Her voice faded away as the name Jason Caldwell echoed in his brain like thunder. Jason Caldwell. First Colorado.

Caldwell?

"Nick? Is something wrong?"

"Who is Jason Caldwell? What does he have to do with First Colorado?"

Miss Sally and Lowdy exchanged tense looks. She set the letter down. "Forgive me, Nick, but it's common knowledge your father financed his ranch with First Colorado, but under steep terms."

Lowdy grunted. "Lot of ranchers opened accounts with 'em when they first came to the area. The bank was eager for business, and the ranchers were eager for loans."

"Because of the winter of '78-'79," Miss Sally interjected.

"I remember that winter." Nick shook his head. "We had cattle freeze to death standing up. I was just a kid, but I remember how tough it was..." And it was the beginning of the end for his pa.

"Caldwell took advantage of their pain," Lowdy said.

"Pa never said names, that I recall. He just blamed *the bank* for the interest rate and the terms." Nick had never heard the name Caldwell until a few weeks ago. Was Jason related to Sierra?

Sarah.

"Jason Caldwell *was* First Colorado," Lowdy growled. "I had good friends lost everything 'cause of doing business with that thief. Worse, he took some of their horses."

"Yes," Miss Sally said. "He exploited their losses. Got richer. Built himself a magnificent home."

"I think the man oughta be in jail."

"Possibly. I kept my business with the banks in Denver. It's been inconvenient at times, but the men I work with, I know I can trust. I couldn't ever say that about Caldwell. Now, First Colorado is selling its branch over in Hell's Half-Acre..."

A wealthy banker in Denver. Named Caldwell. With a beautiful home, stables, world-class horses...and a daughter born to high society.

"Nick, you look white as snow. Are you all right?"

He touched his stomach and tried to figure out the answer. Had her father been the crooked thief who had preyed upon his pa? Caused a good woman to kill herself with stress...and a good man to kill himself with a gun? "I—I am feeling a little peaked right now. I think I just need some breakfast."

"Oh, all right. I'll have Maude fix you something. All we wanted to tell you is that Colorado National is going to buy the First Colorado branch. I'll be sitting on the board. You and the other ranchers in Green County will have a good, honest bank to go to for fair terms. When you're ready."

He heard Miss Sally, but only in the back of his mind. An ember of fury glowing in his gut, he rose to his feet. "Thank you. You two don't mind, I'm gonna head back to the bunkhouse. Grab a biscuit and some honey."

"You do that," Miss Sally ordered. "Get your feet underneath you. Let me know if you need anything. Tonics, a doctor."

"Yes, ma'am, but I'm sure I'll be fine." He forced himself to walk slowly and loosen the fist his fingers kept making.

A fist he'd like to plant square in Jason Caldwell's face.

NICK JUMPED on Dante and rode hard and fast toward the home place. The pounding of the horse's hooves, the wind surging over his face, breathed life into the anger in his gut. It flamed up, and when he saw the house, he whipped Dante with the reins, had the horse careen down the hill, past the cabin, a mile further to the creek...and the towering oak.

He pulled back hard on the reins. Dante skidded to a stop.

Nick stared at a spot on the tree. A scar that was grayed out now. Years ago, it had been a small, white reminder where the bullet had finished off his father. And around it, blood and brain spatters had spelled out the last moments of a good man's life.

Spud, his father's foreman, had found him. And had kept Nick away at first. He'd said a teenage boy needed time to think, not just react. A week later, he'd brought Nick out here.

Now, he dismounted and approached the tree, wondering for the millionth time how a man could lose all his hope. Be so empty that even a kid wasn't enough motivation to keep him fighting.

Spud had pointed at the bullet scar and said, "Nick, I'm gonna tell it to you straight. Your pa gave up. Not just on himself, but on his friends. On you. And that's a cryin' shame. He cheated himself, and he cheated us."

First, they'd gotten behind in the mortgage because of that hard winter. Then Ma had worked herself sick. With her gone, Pa had folded. Let a bank and life beat him. Even though he still had a son to live for.

Spud was right. Pa had cheated them. And the banker had cheated him.

But he should have been smarter. Not signed on to just any deal thrown at him by a greedy, arrogant banker.

"I'll be smarter. And I will get this place up and running." Nick had vowed he'd never give up, back down...or lose hope. There would always be a way better than the one his pa took.

In the meantime, he had the banker's daughter, and he was going to get at least a sprig of revenge.

CHAPTER NINE

"NICK SUGGESTED A DIFFERENT TASK TODAY, SARAH." MISS Sally slid a steaming cup of coffee across the long kitchen table to Sarah and then poured herself one. "We're painting the barn. Tedious work. But it needs a steady hand, especially around the windows and dormers."

Sarah sipped the coffee and savored the warm, nutty flavor. She didn't know if she had liked coffee before, but on this side of the slate, she enjoyed it immensely.

Painting. "Well, it might not be as dangerous as feeding cows and goats. I'm willing to try."

Something mysterious glinted in the woman's violet eyes, and then she half-smiled. "You're not taking this lying down or whining. Good."

SARAH LEARNED something else about her current life: she didn't care for heights. She'd been instructed to take the red and white paint up the scaffold and paint the barn's sides and windows. She moved slowly, with great care. She didn't think she'd ever been on a scaffold before, or if she had, she did not think the experience had been pleasant.

Sarah took one last glance at the ground twenty feet below and swore not to do so again until she was finished. "I'm going to do this as if I'm five feet off the ground. And if this doesn't jog something loose in my brain..." The hope was the only thing keeping her on the scaffold.

WHEN NICK CAME around the corner, Sarah had painted about half the side of the barn, up to a dormer. He stepped over behind a covered wagon and watched her leaning in close to carefully finish off the red around the trim. She was painstaking with the details.

A mischievous idea had sprouted in his mind the night before and he smirked. "Just how involved is she?" Snuffing laughter, he quietly slipped up to the ladder and started easing it down into his hands as he walked backward. Slow and easy. He didn't want the wood to creak and tip her off.

Enormously pleased with this prank that seemed to be flowing smooth as silk, he tucked the heavy, cumbersome ladder beneath his arm and spirited it away behind the barn.

"Now," he said, leaning it against the wall, "where's the best place to watch the fireworks?" He decided on the chicken coop.

SALLY WAS a split second away from hailing Nick when he started removing the ladder. Closing her mouth, she stepped back into the shadows of her porch. "What in the world…?" He looked to be stealing the ladder. *Lord, what is that boy up to? It's not like him to devil someone for no reason...so there must be a reason.* She settled against the log wall of the house, deciding to let this play out, at least for a few minutes. *Maybe he just borrowed the ladder?*

When he skulked away with it, she tossed out the idea. Nick had definitely been sneaking away with the ladder. Sally crossed her arms and waited.

SARAH PAINTED one long section of siding red, and then was ready to change to white paint and a smaller brush for the dormer. She turned to her supplies…and paused. For a moment, it didn't register.

Where's the...?

Unbelieving, she straightened up and scanned the scaffold.

Where was the ladder?

She peered over the edge, and her stomach rolled at the distance. But there was no ladder there, not lying on the ground, or anywhere else nearby. Her heart bolted to a gallop in her chest. Confusion and fear collided in her brain. Somehow, the ladder disappearing equated in her mind with a scaffold about to collapse. She grabbed a support and yelled, "Somebody? Anybody? I need help."

This is a busy ranch. Where in the world is everyone? How can there not be a soul in sight?

"Somebody," she yelled again, louder. "Miss Sally—" *Nick.* She couldn't bring herself to call for him. "April? Gilly?"

"Somethin' amiss, ma'am?"

Sarah sighed and looked down between the boards of the scaffold. Hub peered up at her from the stall window below, a pinch of what looked like genuine concern on his brow.

"Yes, the ladder is missing. I'm stranded up here...and I don't like heights."

Hub ducked inside the barn and momentarily reappeared at the bottom of the scaffold. He surveyed the area. "Well, that's kind of funny." He took his hat off, raked his hands through his sweaty, sandy-colored hair, and replaced the Stetson. "Couldn't have gone far. Just sit tight and I'll round it up."

"Sit tight?" Sarah opted not to say anything sarcastic, though it took a Herculean effort. "Thank you, Hub."

SALLY DRUMMED her fingers on her thigh, glancing at Nick's hiding spot behind the chicken coop. She was glad Hub had been nearby, but this little prank troubled her. Her gaze drifted off to the far fields, and she absently noted a few riders on horseback moving a group of cattle toward the horizon. This behavior was so unlike Nick. She considered yelling and telling Hub where to find the ladder, but decided to be a fly on the wall.

She looked back at Sarah, curious now as to what she might do with her situation. Hang on for dear life and wait for rescue? Or—

The girl turned toward the dormer, paintbrush poised in her hand to paint, but then she froze. Curious, Sally strode to the edge of the porch to see what had the girl's attention.

To GET her mind off the wobbly scaffold and the fact that she was stuck twenty feet in the air, Sarah resolved to finish the dormer. She had to do something, or the panic and fear were going to win. They were looming larger and darker with every breath.

"It's going to be all right, S...S..." A name was so close she could almost pull it out of the shadows. Almost. She gave up. "Sarah. It's going to be all right. Just paint and get your mind off"—she gulped—"the ground."

She dipped the paintbrush in the milky paint, turned toward the dormer.

Something flashed in her mind's eye and she straightened. "It was...it was..." An image?

What?

Yes, an image...

She side-stepped ever-so-carefully to the other side of the window, to the unpainted section of wall, and put the brush to the wood. Sarah couldn't explain it, but she had a vision in her head, and somehow, her hand carried it out. The paintbrush drifted up, down, over. Each stroke a creation of something, pulled from a memory awash in darkness.

She got more paint. She could see the picture in her mind's eye. The brush in her fingers, moving faster and faster, unfurled an image...

SALLY SMILED as she figured out what the girl was doing and walked over to the barn, deliberately not looking in Nick's direction. Pleased with Sarah's apparent breakthrough, she caught Hub as he came around from the back, ladder under his arm. She pressed a finger to her lips and then pointed up. They both stepped back for a better view.

"What's she doing?" he whispered.

"Painting." Then they heard her humming. Sally followed along, nodding, straining to pull the song from her memory. "Für Elise. A beautiful tune." And not one most ordinary folks would know. Common to high society girls, though.

SARAH STEPPED AWAY from the painting, awed by what she'd created, wishing she could view it from further away. Up close, the horse's head, tossed back, his mane flying, his heels kicked up, expressed such joy and freedom. But was the scale right? Had she made any mistakes?

As if in answer, her hand reached out and added some detail to the mane.

"So, you're an artist."

Miss Sally's voice didn't quite break through Sarah's surprise. "I don't know. Am I?"

"From down here, I'd say you are. A very gifted one. Here..." She motioned for Hub to reset the ladder. "Come down so you can see the whole thing."

Hub obliged and steadied the ladder so Sarah could descend...into his arms. She pushed past him absently, too concerned with looking at her work. She immediately saw the flaws, but knew most people wouldn't. "I think I do like it."

"You should," Miss Sally said perfunctorily. "Does this mean you remembered something?"

"No." She shook her head. "I had a flash of something

and the brush in my hand…just felt right. Painting suddenly came to me as naturally as breathing."

"Mighty fine work," Hub said.

"Thank you."

"So fine, we'll leave it." Miss Sally walked away and spoke over her shoulder. "Put some varnish or something over it to protect it and the wood." Looking in the direction of the coop, she added, "Thanks for finding the ladder, Hub."

Puffing out his chest, Hub slid up beside Sarah and dropped an arm around her shoulder. "You're mighty talented, Miss Sarah."

She looked up and wasn't surprised at the winning grin the man wore. His arm around her was another matter. "That is a liberty I have not extended to you." She stepped out from beneath him. "Thank you, though. For the ladder. I was…frightened."

He held the grin, the expression saying he'd win in the end. There was no point in resisting. "Don't like heights, huh?"

The ridiculous question annoyed her and she chose to ignore it. "Where did you find the ladder?"

"Behind the barn."

"Behind the—" As if…

"Almost like somebody moved it on purpose."

She could think of one person who might be so inclined.

CHAPTER TEN

Nick rubbed his scruffy jaw and sighed. He'd watched the show unfold from his vantage point at the coop, and it hadn't turned out like he'd thought it would. He'd thought she'd be stuck. Cry for help. Get humbled a little. He hadn't wanted Hub, of all people, to be the savior, but at least it didn't look as if that had gone in his favor.

He tsked. "She don't look too interested, Hub." Nick was glad, but, of course, only because he liked watching the pretty boy get thrown every now and then. There wasn't a gal in the territory he hadn't tried to dazzle with his smile and flirty mouth. Sarah had set him straight, or so it had appeared.

No, it was really the picture that she'd painted that had ruined Nick's fun. And worried him. It was a beautiful picture of a mustang on the gallop, stretched out, mane and tail whipping in the wind.

The woman had legitimate talent. Did this mean she'd remembered something? Everything?

"Nick, I've been looking for you."

He almost flinched at Miss Sally's icy tone from behind him, but sucked in his bottom lip and turned to her. "Yes, ma'am. You found me."

"Explain yourself."

"Pardon?"

Miss Sally huffed a sigh and raised her chin. Not in the hoity-toity way Sarah did it. No, this was a motion that framed a you-are-on-thin-ice expression. She tossed her silver braid back over her shoulder and dropped her hands on her hips. "I saw you take the ladder."

"Oh..." Yeah, he was in trouble.

"Honestly, what's the matter with you? I've never seen you act like this. Especially toward a woman. I want an explanation. Now."

He laced his fingers together with some force, shoving the leather further down between his fingers. "It was just a joke. She was pretty uppity at the train station, and then she was fussing about the chores yesterday being beneath her."

Which wasn't a lie, exactly. She'd told Angel something pretty close to this, and he'd happened to overhear.

Miss Sally raised a suspicious eyebrow. "Why are you so intent on trying to humble her?"

"I-I'm not really trying—"

"Could it be that because you think she's wealthy or cultured, that you're...well..." She lowered her voice. "You've a distaste for the type of people who took advantage of your father?"

Nick felt his own brow shoot up. Was that part of this? Was that why he was so offended by her and wanted a little revenge? Was he taking this all a little too personally?

"I see I've given you something to think about. I'll

leave it at that." She pointed a long, elegant finger at him. "But no more. Leave her alone."

"Yes, ma'am."

She started to walk away, but stopped, and rounded on him. "She didn't know she could paint. And the first thing she paints is a horse." She locked her gaze on him. "Find out if she can ride. Maybe there's something here, a connection we're missing."

Nick knew he should tell her. Tell Miss Sally everything. He could just open his mouth and spill it all. *I've known who she is all along. She's the daughter of the banker who took everything my pa had. You're right. It's personal. And I'm not quite ready to let her off the hook.*

Forgive me, Lord. Just a little more humbling.

SALLY CLOSED her Bible and stared across her office at nothing. *Why are you being so quiet, Lord? No, it's not You. It's me. I'm distracted. Mostly about Sam, I suppose. He's getting so dark, drifting down a bad road. I'll always ask for Your mercy toward him, Father. But his heart seems to be hardening.*

She shook off the chill from the forlorn thoughts and turned them toward Sarah.

How can I help her if I don't know anything about her? And what in the world is Nick hiding?

She leaned back in her chair and drummed her fingers on her blotter. "All right. With Your permission, then, I'll try something a little more earthly." When she didn't sense disapproval, she grabbed her hat from the corner of her desk and bounded from her chair.

SAM LEANED back from his desk and took a sip of whiskey. "Your request is most surprising."

"Why?" She glanced at the glass in his hand. It was becoming more of a habit, or so she thought. Fanning herself with her hat, she sat down across from him.

"Asking me for help. What, is He on vacation? I can't believe He'd ignore *you*."

"He's not ignoring me." She rotated her shoulders, trying to stop him from annoying her. "There are days it's easier to hear Him than others. That's all. I prayed about this, and I have peace. I think it's what He wanted me to do, after all."

A dark eyebrow ticked up. "Convenient."

"Stop being so difficult. Either help me or not."

He ran his finger around the top of his glass and heaved a heavy sigh. "I suppose, from your perspective, I owe you. After all, I'm here in this"—he motioned to the room around him—"this paradise, because of your request."

"I still say it was better than the alternative."

"Undoubtedly."

"Then why are you always so angry about it?" she snapped.

Both his brows rose. "I'm not the one yelling."

"I'm sorry. He's never been difficult to hear from before. It's not Him, it's me."

Sam chuckled sardonically.

"No," she argued. "We're the ones who get distracted, get too busy for Him. Follow other gods. As you well know."

Sam set down the empty glass and pushed it away. "Let's not delve into that today. What do you need?"

"A private investigator."

"A private investigator?"

"Yes."

"Isn't that a little like Alexander Graham Bell asking to make a phone call…on someone else's phone?"

"Call it what you like, I know what I need. And you know everyone."

"True."

The compliment seemed to put him back to the request rather than the reason for it. "I know several. They have their specialties. Insurance fraud, robbery, missing persons—"

"Missing persons."

"Someone at the ranch?"

"Yes. The girl with amnesia."

"That's interesting. Still, I'm surprised you don't know something—"

"She's a blank slate, so without…" She glanced heavenward.

"Without divine intelligence, you need human intelligence."

"Succinctly put."

"I'll have a man contact you."

"Thank you." She didn't want to dally because that was precisely what she wanted to do, so she rose. "Town seems quiet. I hope you're staying out of trouble." She regretted the compassion that had slipped into her voice. He never reacted well to that.

This time, surprisingly, he didn't respond at all. With a nod, she slipped around her chair and headed for his door.

"You should wear a dress every once in a while, Sally."

She knew what he was saying. She'd felt his eyes on her, appraising her from the moment she'd walked in. "I'm not so svelte anymore. Dresses are cumbersome."

"You're just as beautiful as you ever were. Perhaps more so."

She looked over her shoulder to smile at him, but he was contemplating the empty whiskey glass. So many things she could say. With obedience came joy. Peace. Rebellion only brought heartache. "Living in His will does that for you."

"Well, then, it's a wonder I look as good as I do."

Sally turned away and reached for the doorknob. "Yes, it is a wonder."

SARAH MOPPED up some gravy with a heavenly-tasting biscuit and cautioned herself to watch her appetite. But she couldn't. Something about discovering her hidden gift of painting had kept her heart pounding stronger today, lifted her mood higher. Gave her an appetite. The empty space of her past didn't seem as daunting.

"I can paint," she whispered, "and I think I like horses."

"What did you say?" April asked, leaning a little closer. The dining hall was not a quiet place at mealtime.

"Oh, I was just thinking out loud. I have a skill I didn't know about."

"Yah, I heard. You painted a beautiful picture on the barn. Miss Sally adores it."

That, too, made Sarah smile. She liked being appreciated.

A delicate but clear tinkling sound slowly penetrated all the minds and mouths moving in the hall. The women quieted and focused their attention on Miss Sally, who was standing at the head of her table, rapping a spoon on a tin cup.

Acknowledging she had everyone's attention with a nod, she set the items down and clasped her hands in front of her. "I'm pleased to announce we'll be having a bonfire tonight."

Several of the women in the room cheered, all of them clapped, though many with bewildered expressions. Sarah looked at April. "What's this about?"

April smiled and regarded her with an almost dreamy glimmer in her brown eyes. "You'll see."

"So," Miss Sally continued, "I'll see you all outside at dark."

As DUSK GAVE way to the night, Sarah inched her way to the front of the crowd at the bonfire. She could feel an excitement in the air. Even the more quiet women on the ranch were looking eagerly toward the space in front of the fire. Beside her, in the flickering flames, curiosity danced in the shadows of Polly's face.

Sarah wanted to discuss what was happening with April, but had lost her somewhere after dinner, and she didn't see her in the crowd. She gave thought to going to look for her when Miss Sally emerged from behind the fire. The chattering in the group died almost instantly.

The woman, tall and elegant as ever in her comfortable dungarees, surveyed the crowd. Sarah thought she had such a warm, almost magical glow about her. Something very good had happened or was about to happen, and Sarah listened intently as Miss Sally spoke.

"Thank you all for coming this evening. You know, unity is one of the strengths of our group here at Burning Dress. We all understand how hard life is." She passed a glance over the crowd. "We've all experienced heartbreak, disappointment, hopelessness. And that's what we're here for—to find our hope again. To find the reasons for going on."

Miss Sally shoved her hands into her pockets and, lowering her head, took a moment to gather her thoughts. "Respect." She pointed at the crowd. "You all deserve respect. You are made in the image of our Father, and you are beautiful, unique creations, each and every one of you. Our honoree tonight has something to say about that." She looked into the shadows. "April?"

A moment later, April emerged into the firelight carrying a dress. A somewhat formal one, Sarah noted. Emerald green. Ornately embroidered with pearls. A wedding dress? she wondered.

April turned and faced the audience. "My husband beat me." Her words pressed a silence over the women that was so intense, it raised goosebumps on Sarah's arms. April drifted her fingers over the buttons on the shirtwaist and shook her head. "He called me weak. Frail. Sickly. And I was. I got worse when I married Frederich. The sicker I got, the more he beat me."

Sarah bit down on her bottom lip and scanned the faces of the women nearby. Some of the expressions were stone cold and hard. Others were tense, with mouths downturned, lips thinned. A few of the women blinked back tears. Like Polly.

"I came here barely alive. Miss Sally, Gilly, and Maude brought me back to life." April's eyes shimmered with emotion as she sought the women and gave them each a nod. "I hated my husband. I used to daydream about knocking him in the head and burying him in the garden."

A somber chuckle rumbled through the crowd.

"When I was…healing. Working. Getting stronger…

Miss Sally was telling me about Jesus. About perfect love. And the freedom in forgiveness." She twisted the dress in her hands and sniffled. "I wish my marriage had been better. I wish Frederich had been a better man, but that was not the case. Tonight, it does not matter. I am free. I am free of my hate and my bitterness. I am free from the curse of sin and death. My Savior loves me. He loves me just the way I am. I forgive Frederich. I am even grateful to him. If he had not beat me, I might not have come to Burning Dress Ranch." She slid her gaze to Miss Sally. "And I am so glad I did."

Miss Sally slowly nodded and smiled at April.

"So...I don't need this, because I am the Bride of Christ." She held up the gown, high over her head for everyone to see, and then spun to the fire and cast the dress on the flames. Simultaneously, a cheer went up from the group of women, and they surged past Sarah like a sea tide to hug April, congratulate her, cry with her.

Feeling out of place, wondering what mysteries lurked in her own past, Sarah drifted off to the side.

"The first woman to own this ranch burned her gown."

Sarah turned her head toward Miss Sally, who had stepped up beside her. "Why? Was she abused, too?"

"No. Betrayed would be a better word... The young man she was going to marry turned bad, broke her heart. Her father had warned her he was no good." She shrugged sadly. "Anyway, when the dust settled and her heart was in a million pieces, she promised herself she'd never disobey her father again."

This sweeping decision bothered Sarah for some reason. "Strikes me she put a lot of trust in her father."

"Some fathers"—Miss Sally slid her gaze over to Sarah—"you can do that."

"I suppose. So she burned her dress because...?"

"As a way of remembering to always put Jesus ahead of everything. Even a man."

Sarah's turn to shrug. "I'm sure it's a valuable lesson... I don't think I have anyone I need to forgive."

"Sometimes it's the other way around."

"Meaning...?"

"Sometimes you're the one who needs forgiveness and it's withheld."

Sarah had no comment, as she didn't know if she had any experience with either case. "I-I..."

Miss Sally waved the conversation off. "What I came over here to say was I hired a private detective today. Maybe he can find out something about your past."

"Oh, that was very kind of you." The move surprised Sarah and impressed her deeply. Miss Sally was not about half-measures. In fact, she seemed quite determined to solve the mystery of Sarah. "Thank you. I'm sure I can pay you back at some point."

"We won't worry about that now. Let's find out who you are first."

CHAPTER ELEVEN

Kevin flicked a flame up on the crystal cigar lighter and offered it to his guest. Sean Murphy looked up from his seat, stopped searching for a match in his pocket, and accepted the flame. The cigarillo glowing, Kevin set the lighter back down on his desk and circled back to his seat.

An Irish gangster, Sean was a young man, in his early thirties, and ambition rolled off him in waves. The reason Kevin liked him. "So, to be clear," he said, leaning back in his large, leather office chair, "you know nothing of Sierra's disappearance?" He picked up a pencil and danced it between his fingers.

Sean exhaled smoke, inspected the fine cigar with a look of approval, and shook his head. "Nothing."

Kevin had no choice but to believe him. Neither the Murphys nor the Clantons had anything to gain by lying.

"If we had taken yer girl, ye'd know by now what we want."

The same words spoken by Billy Clanton.

So where had his little bride-to-be gone? Did she really think she could run away and get out of marrying him? No. Kevin was going to get his matrimonial hooks into the countess's royal line if it killed him. Or someone else.

The pencil in his fingers snapped.

Sean chuckled. "I see yer a bit frustrated with the situation. Come down to our pub tonight. I've a gal that can work out all your kinks. On the house." He swiped his bowler up from Kevin's desk and stood. "Ye've done well keeping my boys out of the clink. Least I can do."

"It does pay to have a good attorney on your side. But I may want more than a trollop."

"As in?"

He was thinking of Devonshire. What if the man found Sierra and the situation wasn't to Kevin's liking? As in, she had purposely run away to avoid marrying him and refused to return home—an unacceptable embarrassment. It would be best if Kevin got to her first. "I want you to have a man ready to do a little investigating for me, should I need it."

Sean took a puff on his cigar, watched the smoke swirl as he exhaled. "I think I can oblige ye."

A CROWING ROOSTER greeted Sarah as she left the big house and strode toward the barn. She still had a funny feeling in her stomach this morning, almost like a nervous excitement. She should be angry with Nick. He had to have been the one who took the ladder…but the result had been so redeeming.

She could paint. She could draw. She'd spent an hour last night sketching things in a journal Miss Sally had given her. Random things, but they were familiar. A barn with six gables. A black stallion with a beautiful diamond-shaped blaze on its face. A cat sunning in a window.

Things from her mysterious past? They had to be. Memories would open soon. She was sure of it.

Beside her, April chuckled as she rolled up her sleeves. "You seem to be in a good mood."

"I am, and I'm not exactly sure if I should be, but I can't help it."

The girl frowned, her widow's peak moving with the effort. "You are strange. Why question a good mood? It is better than a bad mood, I suppose."

"I suppose." Sarah shifted her focus from herself to her friend. "You certainly seem...*lighter*, as well."

"Praise God, I have let go of so much bitterness that was polluting my soul. I feel like I could fly. You should give the Lord a chance."

Sarah shrugged. "I don't know that I haven't. I think maybe He's here"—she laid a hand over her heart—"but like so much of my past, I just have a hint, a shadow of Him..." She smiled sheepishly at April. "I want to be happy like you. Seeing you like you are makes me smile."

"I pray you have lots of reasons to smile today. Maybe you will figure out something about you." April squeezed Sarah's shoulder in an affectionate gesture. "But if you don't, know that Jesus has never left you. Maybe you don't remember Him so good, but He has not forgotten you."

Sarah found that encouraging. "Thank you for the reminder."

"*Yah*. Soon, we will talk about it."

They waved at each other and continued in their separate directions. Sarah strode toward the barn, and as she entered, her steps slowed. The smell of manure, horses, hay...she stopped and concentrated on the smells. The butterflies in her stomach flitted about faster. This place made her smile.

A noise pulled her toward a stall on the right. Mr. Bannister was inside it with a horse. He rested a bucket of combs and brushes on a shelf and turned back to the gate. His eyes widened. "Oh, didn't hear you come in. Morning."

"Morning, Mr. Bannister," Sarah said, and she wanted to be angry, but the good mood wouldn't give way. Besides, the horse stole her focus. A sorrel with a broad forehead grumbled at her and stuck his head over the gate for a pat. She stroked his cheek and then noticed a bucket of feed in a wheelbarrow. "Here, boy." She scooped up a handful and offered it to the animal.

The feel of his velvety lips and gruff whiskers pressing on her palm made her smile. Suddenly, an image popped into her head. Or, no, it was more like an experience. She saw her hands brushing down a horse's thick, black mane, felt the strength of the muscles as she scratched its neck. But it was only a flash, a tidbit of...a memory?

She looked at Nick. He'd been watching her, but he returned to the bucket, brusquely sorting through the items. "Here, hold this." He passed her the bucket. "We're gonna take Patches here out and pretty him up for Miss Sally. And you can call me Nick. Everyone but you does."

Sarah noted his movements were sharp and almost rough as he hooked a lead line to the mare and led her from the stall.

"Do you always handle the horses that way, *Nick*? Like an untrained stable boy?"

Nick stopped as if he'd come to the edge of an unexpected cliff. "*Stable boy?*" He shook his head and led the horse over to a hitching post. "If you don't beat all." Really agitated now, he wrapped the rope around the post like he was trying to hurt it. "Miss High-and-Mighty. You'd think you'd—" He stopped.

"I'd what?" What had he started to say? An insult?

"Nothing." He took the bucket from her. Muttering under his breath, he pulled a brush from the bucket and dragged it over the horse.

Sarah drifted around the barn, trying to ignore the surly cowboy and take in the comforting scents, the feeling of peace the barn gave her. Her attention, however, kept whipping back to Nick and his abrupt, snappy movements with the brush. The horse grumbled and shook his head, communicating his disapproval.

He'll start prancing in a minute, Sarah thought. *He doesn't like the way Nick is handling this.* Finally, she gave up and followed either instinct or memory. "Here, let me." She pushed him out of the way and took the brush from him. "You're too rough." She began brushing the animal, a little too fast at first, then she slowed down, pleased with the feel of the tool in her hand. It felt good. Right. She stroked the horse's side with her other hand. This felt right, too. She drifted her fingers over the muscles in the gelding's shoulder—

"You remembering anything?"

"Maybe. I don't know." It was maddening, almost as if her memory was so close, it was just barely hiding in the shadows. With a little more light—

"Let's find out if you can ride." Nick held a saddle blanket out for her.

At first, Sarah didn't understand, then it dawned on her that he wanted her to saddle the horse. She put the brush away and gently laid the blanket on the animal's back. She dallied for a moment, her hands still clutching the corners of the blanket. *Something. So close...*

"Next, Your Worship, the saddle."

She scowled at him, annoyed with his odd behavior and constant interruptions. "Where are they?"

"Turn around."

She did as ordered and faced a wall of posts, several of them holding saddles. "Does it matter which one?"

He squinted at the tack, as if pondering the question. "Third one from the end." She grabbed it, slung it over the horse...and paused.

"Grab the cin—"

She tossed up a hand. "Shh. Let me see if I can do this."

He threw up his hands in surrender and backed off. "Just hope you have a better handle on this than milking the cow."

She shot him another glare, but then pushed him out of her mind. She took the cinch in her right hand. *What now?*

"Maybe if I don't think about it too much." Sarah just started moving. Her body did seem to know what to do. She pulled, yanked, buckled. When Nick handed her the bridle, she took it in such a way that easily allowed her to slip it on the horse and the bit into his mouth. Holding one of the reins, she stepped back. "I did it."

"Yeah, you did." A troubled dip in Nick's brow got her attention.

"What?"

He blinked and straightened up. "You can saddle a horse. Let's see if you can ride, Princess." He walked past her, and it was all Sarah could do not to kick him in the seat of his pants.

"If I can saddle one, I can ride. I'm sure of it." *And you'll eat my dust, Nick Bannister.*

NICK HELD the gate open to the corral and made a grand, sweeping—mocking—gesture for Sarah to enter, the gelding trailing behind her. She cut her eyes at him, the heat in them capable of singeing his eyebrows, and walked out into the center of the ring.

He was using sarcasm to hide his concern. What if a few minutes in the saddle brought it all back? He half-expected her to look at him any second now and yell, *You're that cowboy who hates my horses.* The thought gave him a shiver.

Shaking it off, sort of, Nick closed the gate and dropped the rope latch in place. Hub drifted up and draped his arms over the top rail. "You trying to get her killed?"

"*She* picked Otis, not me."

"You tell her anything about that horse?"

"I guess she'll figure it out." *Surely the woman can remember how to ride...*

Hub turned and leaned on the fence. "What is it with you and her? I ain't never seen you pick on anybody before, least ways none of the girls here."

Nick plucked a looped rope off the fence post and dropped all but one end to the ground. "Ah, it's just the way she is." He started winding the rope up again, just for something to do. "She acts like she's better than everybody else."

"Might be she is."

"Nope. I don't buy that at all."

"Well, regardless..." He slapped Nick on the shoulder

and pointed at the girl in the center of the corral, about to take the saddle. "You'd best keep an eye on her."

Nick slowed his hands on the rope and put his attention on Sarah as she climbed into the leather. Otis stood quietly, waiting for a tug on the reins or a nudge to his side. Sarah seemed to debate what to do next, then she gently tapped the gelding on the sides with her heels. His head came up a little and his ears twitched.

"Uh-oh," Hub whispered.

Nick put the rope back on the post and slowly lifted the loop on the gate.

Sarah huffed and kicked the horse a little harder, at the same time slapping his flank with the reins.

Every muscle in Otis's body tightened, and then he exploded like a stick of dynamite. He leaped straight up into the air, then went to seesawing his body. Sarah squealed and clawed for the saddle horn, but Otis released a kick full of an impressive amount of power. The girl backflipped right out of the saddle and landed in the dirt, face down.

Nick hurried over to her, Hub on his heels. They helped her to her feet as she was spitting dirt and cursing them under her breath.

"You all right, ma'am?" Hub asked, sounding oh-so-concerned. Nick cut his eyes at the man, wishing he'd go back to work.

Wiping her mouth, Sarah spat again and pushed the cowboys off her. She had a glare for both of them, but it ended on Nick. "You knew he was going to do that, didn't you?"

He grinned sweetly. "Maybe you can't ride."

Her pretty face hardened, picked up an edge.

Uh-oh.

Nick had a feeling he'd just poked a bear.

"Challenge accepted." She pushed gruffly through them, gathered up the recalcitrant horse, and looked him in the eye. "You threw me because you could. You won't do it again."

The horse's ears went down and out in confusion. They weren't pinned to his head, and Nick thought maybe the horse actually got the gist.

"Fool me once," Sarah muttered, stepping into the saddle. This time, she didn't hesitate. She nudged the horse with her heels and used her hips to imply what she wanted. Otis obeyed smartly. In only a few seconds, Sarah was trotting the horse around in a big circle, and around a chagrined Nick. Hub was smiling that stupid, huge grin of his and clapping his gloved hands.

"There ya go, girl. That's how you ride."

Miss Sally strode up, nodding in appreciation, and rested her hands on the top rail. "Seems we have another hand. I've never seen Otis take to a new rider so easily."

"Oh, he threw me the first time." Sarah trotted over to Miss Sally and pulled Otis up.

The boss lady patted the horse's nose. "Just the first time?"

"He's a smart horse. He sensed my confusion and took advantage of it." She sent an accusing glance at Nick as he and Hub joined the ladies. "I had to set him straight."

"Well, that's fine." Miss Sally nodded at Hub. "Run into town today with Gilly and pick up that load of lumber, if you would. Nick, what do you think about you and Sarah looking for strays?"

Nick sensed another test here and nodded. "Reckon it would be a good chance to show her the main trails."

"Yes, she needs to learn her way around. You're comfortable with the plan, Sarah?"

For an instant, Nick thought she might balk, but she patted the horse's neck and smiled. "I think I'd enjoy that."

He had the sense she wanted to add something like *even if Nick comes,* but she didn't. He nodded his agreement. "I'll get Dante."

CHAPTER TWELVE

THE MORE THEY RODE ACROSS GREEN HILLS, MEADOWS spattered with brilliant wild flowers, and the tops of mesas with spectacular views, the more something soared in Sarah's heart. She felt so free…so relieved to be in the saddle. And it made her want to send up a thank you to heaven.

"You okay?" Nick asked, pulling up beside her. "You look…happy."

She couldn't stop a grin. "Yes. It feels nice riding. Like I've done it before. Maybe a lot." She gazed out over the prairie of rolling, green hills. Memories were so close to surfacing. She was sure of it. "I think there are horses in my life. I know there are."

Nick grunted. "Well, let's check out Devil's Canyon. Usually find a few strays in there."

As they emerged from the grass onto a road, he paused and looked off into the distance. Sarah tracked his gaze. "What is it?"

"Nothing." But he didn't move.

"Must be something."

He shrugged. "My old home place is down there."

Sarah wanted an excuse to stay in the saddle a little longer. "Is it far? Can you show me?"

Her request snatched his gaze to her, and for a moment, she thought she saw an unfriendly glint in his eye. But he smiled and said, "Sure. Why not?"

They kicked their horses up to a lope, and a few minutes later, they topped a hill. A warped, ramshackle cabin sat alone and forgotten in the midst of a pretty valley of tall, green grass. A healthy creek cut through it. Nick didn't pause long to study it, but hurried down to the hitching post and dismounted. Sarah followed, curious about the reason for Nick's suddenly edgy mood.

"You grew up here?" she asked, wrapping the reins around the post.

"I did." He turned and waved his hand over the green hills. "Six hundred acres. Nothing compared to Burning Dress, but it's plenty for getting a good start."

"It looks like fine land." She wasn't lying. There was an abundance of emerald grass waving in the breeze, and plenty of water. "If you grew up here"—she turned to the house—"why is it such a mess?"

Nick's lips tightened into a tense line and he stomped into the cabin. Sarah was getting tired of walking on eggs. She followed him in and looked around the dingy, broken home. The cowboy was leaning back on the mantel, arms crossed, surveying the room.

"My pa lost this place to the bank. I bought it back about a year ago, but it took me a while. And I've still got a few mortgage payments to make."

She drifted her fingers over the counter in the

kitchen and looked at the dust on her fingers. "Apparently. It's yours now, though. If you have a ranch, why are you working for Miss Sally?"

He tilted his head and glared at her so hard she almost took a step back. What was the matter with the man? If anyone should be angry about something, she could fuss about the missing ladder.

"It took everything I had to get the mortgage payments caught up and the back taxes paid. Now, I'm saving up for repairs, operating capital, a herd. It's gonna be a while. Some of us aren't born with silver spoons."

"Meaning I was?" How would he know?

He pushed off the mantle. "Just sayin'. I'm gonna go check on some outbuildings."

Sarah didn't try to stop him. Maybe his slow-blossoming dream was at the core of his sour mood. She surveyed the room, peeked in the bedrooms on each side of the fireplace. Empty and just as dusty, but full of more cobwebs. She thought she heard something rattle in the second bedroom and quickly shut the door.

The room, even in its present mess, struck her as inviting. The windows on the front of the home were large and lit it well. It would be easy to cook in the kitchen. Lots of room and natural light. She tried to imagine Nick here as a young boy, perhaps sitting in front of the hearth, shooting marbles.

He'd said his father had lost the ranch to the bank. Hard times? Alcohol? Any number of reasons a man fails at something, she supposed. It had probably been difficult for the son to watch. And just where were his parents? Considering the way he was acting, she suspected they were both gone.

She glanced out the window and caught sight of him

fiddling with a long piece of grass and staring out over his land. Dreaming about his future here? She took a step closer to the window and kicked a coffee can.

An idea struck her, and she picked it up.

NICK TORE the blade of grass in half and let it fall to the ground. Mortgage payments, cost of repairs to the house and barn, a small herd, some grain and hay for winter. It all took money. He rotated his shoulders, began strolling around the warped outbuildings, wishing things would move faster. But the lie he was treating like a prank on *Sarah* was going to wind up biting him in the bum. He'd best tell her and Miss Sally the truth. He didn't have to confess everything, but he could give them enough to get her home.

He'd thought this morning he'd draw it out a little longer, but something about watching her ride, finding her way around a horse again, handling the animal like she'd been born in the saddle—well, he knew it wouldn't be long before she remembered everything. Best to get out from under it now.

He spun on his heel and marched toward the house. *I'll just tell her she looks familiar. I've seen her. Denver. The train station.*

He jogged up the steps into the house.

Or maybe at a restaurant. Or I'll say as little as possible, Lord, then I'm not really lying.

He burst into the home and froze. Sarah jerked away from the mantle and stepped back, hands tucked behind her back. "You like it?"

She'd gathered a bunch of wildflowers, bright yellow

daisies, pink roses, and some violets, stuffed them into the coffee can, and set the arrangement in the middle of the fireplace mantle. She'd decorated his home.

She had decorated *his* home. Of all the people...

For an instant, he was so angry he could have throttled the woman, but then he saw the bright white and yellow daisies his mother used to put in that very place. The fury melted away and left only emptiness. He missed her. He missed those years.

He missed his father.

Sarah's face fell and she inched back. "I just thought I'd make it homey."

"It was a foolish waste of time. Flowers don't make it a home again." But he did like them. He wandered over and touched a daisy. The flowers reminded him of good times, better days. Summers that never seemed to end. Cutting hay and laughing with his pa. So many good memories...if only he could forget that one final, awful day.

"They help create a vision of what could be here," she said softly. "It's called hope. You have to hope for something."

He lowered his hand and stared down at the floor. "I have hope. It's just going to take forever." He rested his hands on his hips and came back to the flowers. "Why did you do this?"

Her mouth worked silently for a moment before she could eke out any words. "I was just being nice." She sounded confused, but then her tone changed, sharpened. "You don't know how to be gracious, do you?" Arms folded tight, she spun and stomped out to the porch.

Nick scratched his head, readjusted his hat. He'd

made a mess of appreciating a simple gesture of kindness. Sarah didn't know who he was and likely didn't have anything to do with her pa's financial shenanigans. He'd raised a snooty daughter, but that was the father's fault, not Sarah's.

Feeling like a cad, he plucked a daisy from the can and walked it out to her. "What do you hope for?"

Her brow rose in surprise, but she took the flower and offered a slight smile. "Besides my memory?"

He flinched. "Yeah, I guess that was a stupid question."

She twirled the flower around in her fingers. "I hope it comes back." Her gaze drifted off. "And I hope I'll be glad when it does."

Sarah looked so forlorn in that moment, Nick very nearly reached out and brushed a shimmering, strawberry-colored strand of hair behind her ear. He caught himself and glared at his hand as if it were a disobedient child. This was all turning into one big, confusing mess. "I've got things to do. I'm sure you'll find your way back." With that, he pushed past her and headed for his horse.

NICK DIDN'T EXACTLY TAKE his time getting back, but you could have knocked him over with a feather when he rode up to the corral and Sarah was there pulling the saddle off Otis. He'd almost turned back to get her, just in case she took a wrong trail. "How did you—?"

She glared at him as she tossed the saddle over the top rail. "Beat you? Possibly because I'm not stupid, Otis is a fast horse, *and* I can ride. Well." She slapped the saddle as if she wished it were him. "How dare you? How could you just leave me?"

Holy cow, if that high-and-mighty tone of hers didn't make him want to spit nails. "You were only a mile out from the main road, Your Worship."

The woman literally stomped her foot in anger. "What if I'd gotten lost?"

Calmly, simply, he said, "I would have found you."

The words seemed to carry too much weight. Flustered, huffing, she stormed off.

Nick hung his head, tapped his fingers on the saddle horn. *That tone of hers, Lord. Just when I think I should do the right thing, just when I know I will, Her Highness spouts off—*

"Riles you some, doesn't she?" Miss Sally said, and it was not a question.

"Her tone does. I could almost tolerate her if..." *If she'd keep putting flowers on the mantel.* "If she didn't act like she owned the world."

"Did you really leave her out there alone?"

"I was going to go back for her." *At least I was thinking seriously about it.* "I wouldn't have let anything happen to her."

"I did say she needed to learn her way around. Did riding today jog anything loose in her memory?"

"I don't think so."

Miss Sally released a long sigh. "Well, I've hired a private investigator. He'll be here in the next few days. I would imagine he'll want to talk to you."

He reined the horse around to face her. "Why me?"

"You met her at the train station. Maybe you'll say something that will help him."

Nick scratched his ear to buy a moment to think. A detective might be good. He could find out Sarah was Sierra Caldwell, and maybe Nick wouldn't come into it at all.

Miss Sally stroked Dante's nose. "Is there anything you want to tell me?"

The look she gave him suggested she knew something was going on here. Maybe the detective would settle things, though, and Nick could keep his mouth shut. "I guess not, ma'am."

"All right. I'll see you in the morning."

He tapped the brim of his hat and rode into the barn.

SALLY RESTED her elbows on her desk, on each side of her Bible, and prayed. "Oh, Father, quiet my mind and reveal to me something that will help those two." She unlaced her fingers and opened her Bible. Immediately, her eyes fell on Genesis Chapter 42 verse 7: *Joseph saw his brothers and recognized them, but he acted as a stranger to them and spoke roughly to them. Then he said to them, 'Where do you come from?'*

Sally pulled back from the book. The verse quickened her heartbeat. "He knows her." She pressed a hand to her mouth. "That's it, isn't it, Lord? Nick knows who Sarah is?"

It made sense and explained some of his behavior. An old flame? Had she jilted him? Or perhaps she was a Blue Blood and Nick didn't care for her family? Was he trying to get back at her for some wrong she'd done him? Regardless, he'd kept a pretty big secret, and Sally was disappointed in him. "Unless he has his reasons." Until she knew everything, she would give Nick the benefit of the doubt. That didn't mean she wouldn't ask some questions.

She rose from her desk and looked heavenward. "At least that's a start. I'll see what I can do."

SALLY WENT for a ride and timed it to stumble upon Nick and Lowdy out on what they called Angel Creek. Some old legend the Utes in the area told about seeing a beautiful angel with white wings and silver hair drinking water there. The story always made Sally smile.

She hailed the men and rode Patches up to them. "Afternoon, boys. About ready to call it a day?"

"Gonna move this group here"—Lowdy pointed at the small herd—"over to H8 and then we're done."

"Good." Miss Sally looked at the several female hands out, keeping the herd moving. Sarah was among them, but Sally sensed the tension between the girl and Nick. "Lowdy, can you spare Nick here?"

"Sure." Lowdy grinned at the young man. "He's in the way, anyhow." With a wink, the cowboy nudged his horse up to a quick trot and headed back toward the cattle.

"So, Nick..." Sally pressed her knees in, and the horse responded to the gentle touch, moving forward at a lazy walk. "I was wondering."

He urged his horse on and kept Sally's pace. "Yes, ma'am."

"You were in Denver a few months back, weren't you?"

She detected the slightest pause in his answer. "Yes, ma'am. To visit my brother."

"You said he owns a saloon?"

"Yes, ma'am."

She grunted. He didn't meet Sarah in a saloon. "What's Denver up to these days?"

"Ah, lots of steakhouses. Operas. We saw a good show."

"Did you?"

"Yes, ma'am. A comedy called Circus of Fools. The main actor fell down a lot. He was pretty funny."

"Do anything else?"

The pause was longer this time, but she let him answer at his pace. "Looked at some horses. You know me. Horses, cattle, ranches. If I get a chance, I'll look."

Well, the girl was no rancher, but Sally heard something in Nick's voice. He'd phrased his answer carefully. She wouldn't push. Not yet. Not until she knew why he was hedging. "How are things going with Lowdy? Do you feel you're learning a lot?"

"I do. I really do. About cattle. About range management…"

"But?"

"Ah, it just makes me wish my situation could move along faster."

"I'm not trying to get rid of you, but why can't it?"

"Money." He shrugged. "I'm in a good position keeping the mortgage payments up, and I don't owe much more, but it's going to take a while to get the operating capital I need."

"You can always consider either a partner or a bank loan."

He shivered. "I don't know. Either way, I'm beholden to somebody, and I'd rather do this on my own."

"Then remember, slow and steady wins the race. Keep working. Keep saving up."

He sighed heavily and nodded.

"Speaking of races…" She grinned at the cowboy. "Race you back to the barn." And she was off, flying over the prairie and enjoying the wind beneath her wings.

LATER, as the evening waned and the girls had returned to their dorms, Sally went looking for Sarah. She found her on the back portico, staring down at Sally's favorite swing, now awash in silvery, summer moonlight. All around them, the fireflies did their flashing, blinking air dance. Crickets and frogs sang and twanged like banjo strings.

"Lovely evening, isn't it?"

Sarah jerked at the interruption."Oh, yes. It is."

"My apologies. I didn't mean to startle you."

"No, I was lost in—watching—I mean, the lightning bugs. They fascinate me."

"One of a jillion miracles our Father has created for us."

"You..." Sarah turned to her. "You are an amazing woman, Miss Sally. To run this place the way you do. So well."

"Oh." Sally shrugged, a little embarrassed. "When you find the purpose the Lord has called you to, He's honor-bound to bless you. It would be unjust of Him to do otherwise."

"I almost envy you. You talk about God as if you meet with Him on a daily basis."

"I do."

The girl blinked, as if she didn't understand. "I wish I could talk to Him and find my past. My purpose."

"What's stopping you?"

"I-I, well, it's just that, I don't know if I ever talked to Him before. I don't remember."

Sally had come out here to ask Sarah some questions about Nick, but the conversation had taken a turn to her favorite subject and she thanked the Lord for the chance to share.

"His word says He'll never leave us or forsake us." Sally slapped the log rail. "We walk away from Him, but like any loving parent, He's always waiting to welcome His child back home."

"But what if I'm an awful person? Or I don't believe in Jesus and God...?" She faded off.

Sally smiled. "Do you really think that? That you don't believe?"

The girl frowned. After a moment, she shook her head. "I don't feel alone. Is that God?"

"Yes, my dear. His word says there is no place you can go He's not there. Even on the other side of amnesia." She tucked a strand of hair behind Sarah's ear in a motherly gesture. "Draw close to Him. Talk to Him. Read His word. And then, whether you find your past or not, you'll have all you need."

Feeling she'd said enough for the time being, Sally retired to her room and sat on her balcony for a spell. A beautiful full moon hovered high overhead, casting silver light over the ranch, so bright she knew she could read her Bible by it, if she wanted.

Instead, she sat back and tried to listen for His voice and ponder what she suspected about Nick. Not surprisingly, the Lord laid a new thought on her heart: to cancel the private detective.

"I just hired him, Father. He'll be here soon."

They won't get the answers they need there.

She pondered the meaning of this change, but it was an exercise in futility. She never figured out the Lord's plan until He wanted her to. Besides, on occasion, events had seemed to change His mind, or at least the steps on how to bring about His will. Nodding, she rose to her feet. "All right, Lord. I'll send a telegram tomorrow unhiring him. Anything else?"

Then shall the young women rejoice in the dance, and the young men and the old shall be merry...

"Jeremiah 31. Verse 13." She scratched her head. "You want us to have a party?" That didn't seem quite right. "I've no doubt You'll clear it up for me."

CHAPTER THIRTEEN

A PEDDLER'S WAGON HAD ROLLED INTO THE RANCH DURING the day and created quite a stir. Sarah and the women in her crew, Maria, Molly, and Patsy, rode over the hill and gasped when they saw the merchant. He was passing out clothing, brushes, jewelry, and tools to anxious hands. The girls thundered toward him, as eager as everyone else to see his wares.

As they drew close, a basket full of squirming critters grabbed Sarah's attention. She trotted up, swung down, and nearly dove into a mob of barking, panting, licking, black-and-white speckled puppies. Laughing, she picked one up and tried to hold on to the squiggling body while she wrapped her reins around the wagon's rear wheel.

"Pure-bred English Shepherds, ma'am."

Sarah looked over at a man in a yellow-and-black checked suit. He rolled his bowler off his head, down his arm, and caught it in his hand with a bow. "Sheamus O'Herlihy, supplier of odds and ends and everything in between."

The squirming puppy in her arms licked her face,

demanding her attention, and she laughed again. "Oh, they're precious. Just precious."

"Only two dollars for one. Make mighty fine companions and herding dogs."

"Oh, I would love to have one, but..." *When my memory comes back, I'll have to leave. What if I can't take him with me? What if I already have a dog? What if I stay here? Can I keep a dog in our dormitory?* "Well, I'm just not very settled right now."

The man tipped his hat in understanding as he dropped it back on his head and turned again to the clamoring group behind him. Regretfully, Sarah put the puppy back with his litter mates and led her horse to the barn, head down, her heart a little heavy.

Did she have a dog somewhere? Had she ever raised a puppy? Would she? For some reason, the animal drove home the pain of the waiting Sarah was doing. Waiting on her memory. Waiting to learn what skills she had and which ones to learn. Waiting for answers. Did she live on a farm like the one she'd sketched? Did she have her own horse?

The questions were maddening, but her conversation last night with Sally had reawakened her faith. She'd gone to bed and prayed for Jesus to take her worries. She certainly wasn't accomplishing anything by hanging on to them.

"So, I wait, Lord," she said aloud as she led the horse to the last stall. "You've got a plan for me. Help me find it."

NIGHT AFTER NIGHT, Sarah and April had sat next to Polly, and the girl barely said two words to them. They had tried drawing her into their conversations repeatedly, to no avail. She talked softly and in short sentences, kept her head down, and didn't mingle.

Sarah was considering not even trying tonight. But when Polly smiled at them as they joined her at the table, Sarah nearly stumbled. *Polly is smiling.* Stunned, Sarah settled into her seat and returned the pleasant expression. "Good evening, Polly. You look—"

"Beautiful," April interjected, her eyebrows nearly arched up to her widow's peak. "*Yah.* She glows. You agree?"

"I do."

Polly nodded and her smile broadened. "I will be leaving Burning Dress to return to my family."

"Oh, that's wonderful," Sarah said, a little jealous. "I assume. You look very happy about it." And she wondered again why the girl was here in the first place.

"Yes, I am very happy. I missed my brothers and sisters." As if Polly knew they had questions, she said, "I have told no one but Miss Sally why I came to be here. I was ashamed."

April snorted. "You should know by now we all have our reasons for being here."

"I have learned this, so I will tell you. I came here because my father sold me to a man here in Wyoming. I thought I was to be his wife. He wanted me to…to…"

"We get it," April nodded. "He did not want you for himself alone."

Polly nodded. "Yes. And I would not entertain his customers. He beat me, made me sleep in a shack, but I escaped." She cast her eyes toward Miss Sally, two tables over. "I was lost and wandering out on the prairie. Miss Sally found me and brought me here."

"She just happened upon you?" Sarah thought it

possible, of course, but so little seemed to be random or accidental when Miss Sally was around.

"Yes. And here I have learned to farm. Now, my brother and sister are coming for me. Miss Sally found them in San Francisco and paid for their passage here. She has also assisted us in establishing a homestead. We are all very happy and grateful."

"My, that's so generous of her." Sarah was once again moved by the woman's initiative to not just take in strays, but help them put their lives back together. Going beyond teaching them skills, but stepping in to put families in touch. Would Sarah have the same end result?

DINNER WAS, as usual, a feast of wonderful, satisfying food, and Sarah chided herself for the amount of mashed potatoes she'd eaten. She was wondering if her pants were getting tighter when Miss Sally rose and once more tapped on a tin cup. "Ladies, your attention, please." The room quieted instantly. "The merchant committee in town has decided to throw a dance next Saturday night at the Elks Lodge." Some giddy, happy gasps and applause escaped from the women. "You're all welcome, except for those of you who have been here less than a month."

Sarah clearly heard a few disappointed moans. Perhaps she should have been one of them, but she wasn't sure what she thought about seeing a bunch of strangers and dancing with them. Did she dance?

Miss Sally came over and sat down across from her, a playful smile on her lips. "Do you? Dance, Sarah?"

The timing of the question befuddled her for the moment. "Uh, I-I was just wondering that very thing."

"I'll make an exception for you. You should go to the dance. You never know what might knock something loose in that stubborn noggin of yours."

She had a point. "I'm willing to try."

Miss Sally tilted her head. Mischief glimmered in her pretty, violet eyes. "One dance with the right handsome cowboy might bring it all back."

Oh, Lord, could you make it that simple? "Possibly."

April leaned into the conversation, chuckling. "A dance with the wrong handsome cowboy wouldn't be so bad, either."

SARAH ENTERED the Elks Hall and smiled at the sudden rush of lights, music, and swirling, colorful dresses. Much of the crowd clapped in time as the band played a lively tune to which dozens of couples were dancing. A tall, bean-pole of a man with a glistening, bald head was half-yelling, half-singing directions to his audience. Sarah wondered at their intricate maneuvers as they bowed, dipped, locked elbows, and spun.

"Miss Sarah, I'd be honored for a dance." Hub removed his hat and bowed, giving her a winning, toothy grin. She hesitated, but the dancers looked as if they were having the time of their lives.

"I don't know how," she yelled over the noise.

"You do what Jack up there tells you to do." Hub carelessly handed his hat to a boy in suspenders who was passing by, and took Sarah's hand. "It'll be fun. I promise."

They left the boy standing there with a perplexed frown and plunged into the crowd. In only a matter of seconds, Sarah was laughing breathlessly as she tried to follow the commands to circle left, promenade, do-si-do, and so many others. Most of the time, she was a half-second behind and going in the wrong direction, but that added to the fun. Everyone was dancing energetically and having a wonderful time.

When the song ended, the room erupted in cheers, but the men quickly headed for the tables to round up punch for their ladies. Fanning herself, amazed how warm she was, Sarah eyed a cup passing by and Hub laughed at her.

"Would you like some punch, Miss Sarah?"

"I would adore some. Thank you."

He winked. "Be right back."

He disappeared into the crowd and Sarah exhaled. She was glad she'd come. This might be fun, after all. Though she hoped Hub didn't try to monopolize her time. She wouldn't want to give him the wrong impression.

The band had taken a break and the room vibrated with the steady hum of chatting men and the trill of feminine giggles. Sarah scanned the faces, surprised she wasn't able to locate any of the ladies from the Burning Dress.

"There's no way I'll go for a loan. Look what happened to my pa."

Nick? Sarah inched a little closer to a group of men to her right, surrounding the ranch hand. She shouldn't eavesdrop, but certainly they didn't expect any privacy in the middle of a party.

"First Denver sold out," a man said. "It's a good bunch of folks running the bank now. And Miss Sally's on the board."

"True, she did mention that," Nick said.

Sarah heard a softening in his voice, as if the idea could grow on him.

"Folks'll get a fair shake now. No bandits like Caldwell running it."

A path to a table covered in pastries opened up and Sarah nonchalantly drifted to it, moving even closer to Nick's circle of advisers.

"I don't know," he said. "The paperwork is hard. Gotta have a business plan and all. Figure the stock yields, expenses—"

"You're learning all that now."

Sarah recognized that voice. Lowdy. Burning Dress's foreman.

"Yeah. I am. I'll think about it. Right now, I think I'll have a cupcake." He turned from the group and sidled up beside Sarah. She didn't look at him but pondered, instead, the array of baked goods.

She sensed he was well aware of her presence—as she was his—but didn't acknowledge him as she reached for a sugar cookie.

He cleared his throat. "You haven't said a word to me since—"

"Since you left me alone"—her hand froze—"on the prairie with the coyotes and the Indians."

"Now that's kind of an exaggeration. You were one hilltop away from the main road."

"That's a bit of an exaggeration." She plucked a petit fours instead from the table and turned to him. "I didn't know that. What if I'd been the kind of girl who spooks easily? You know, the fragile kind."

"You ain't fragile."

She tilted her head, wondering if that was a compliment.

He tugged on his collar. "Anyway, I do feel bad about leaving you out there. I don't know what made me..."

Miss Sally appeared from nowhere and elbowed him in the ribs, motioning to the dance floor. "Girls do a lot of forgiving on the dance floor. Wouldn't you agree, Sarah?"

Sarah frowned, surprised at the woman's almost magical appearance, and unhappy about being maneuvered into a dance. But Jack was taking his place on the stage, ready to call another tune. It *had* been a lot of fun.

Grudgingly, Nick asked, "Would you, uh, allow me a dance?"

"Dance with whomever you please," she said without looking at him.

Out of the corner of her eye, she saw his brows crash together with irritation, but Miss Sally urged him with a stern look to persevere. He sighed and tried again, in a more pleasant tone. "No, I meant...would you like to dance with me?"

She looked around. Hub was still in the punch line. The band was stirring up what she assumed would be another lively gaited soiree, but shook her head. Only, somehow it flowed into a nod. "All right." She looked around for something to do with her petit fours and Miss Sally took it.

"I love these. Need to get Maude to cook them for us out at the ranch."

"Thank you." Inexplicably a little nervous, Sarah gave Nick her hand, and as they stepped onto the dance floor, the music began for a gentle waltz.

"What the heck?" Nick said.

Both of them clearly feeling awkward, their steps faltering, he shrugged a shoulder, raised his other hand, and waited for her response. The first strains of *Beau-*

tiful Dreamer touched her heart, made her want to dance. She hesitated only an instant and stepped into his arms.

Nick pulled her closer, and the world suddenly fell away. His brown eyes softened, warmed. She felt the heat from his hand holding hers, his arm around her. They stepped and twirled, his lead smooth, strong, comforting.

"This feels familiar," she said, her voice husky with emotions she couldn't describe.

His brow rose a little. "I don't know about familiar, but it's nicer than I thought it'd be." His gaze…seemed to drink her in.

Sarah blinked. She wasn't sure if they were talking about the same thing. "I meant the dance…" *Didn't I?* The weight of his hand on her waist was spellbindingly pleasant. She swallowed and drifted her fingers from his shoulder down a little lower on his arm to feel the muscle move.

The lulling, haunting tones of the fiddle urged her to close her eyes and dream…and feel. Everything about this moment was something she wanted in her mind forever. A memory she would never let go of.

"I'm sorry I barked at you…over the flowers."

His apology pulled her back to a moment that made fairy tales seem possible. "Why did you?"

Why did I?

Staring down into her pretty, glimmering green eyes lined with soft, thick lashes, Nick couldn't quite recall. Why had he been angry with her?

Her hair was down, and it flowed in long, red-tinged,

golden waves that could distract a man right out of his boots.

"Um..." She'd asked a question. "Oh, yeah. I guess I was a little caught off guard. I have a lot of good memories from my home, but a couple of truly bad ones. My ma used to put flowers in that exact spot and..." He faded off, unsure of how to deal with the moment and the question.

"So, that's why you left me? You wanted to be alone?"

Well, that just made him sound like a spiteful sissy. "No—yeah, no, I mean... I was just angry about a lot of things, and you were going to catch the brunt of it if I didn't leave."

"Oh. Well, then, if my choice was ride back with a surly cowboy or wander about in slight panic, yes, I see the favor you did me."

He nearly stopped dancing. "Panic? Were you afraid?"

Perhaps his honest concern showed. She shook her head and let a wry smile break. "Not really. I knew we weren't far from the ranch. It was disconcerting at first, but I do have a fine sense of direction."

"Well, I'm sorry, and I won't do it again."

"That would be appreciated."

The song was winding down, and Nick caught sight of Hub standing on the sidelines, holding two dainty glasses of punch in his hands and a murderous scowl on his face. "Could I have one more dance?" Nick asked hastily. "They usually do two slow ones back-to-back."

Sure enough, the band went right into Annie Laurie. Sarah nodded, her cheeks flushing a little. "All right. Just one. I'm sure Hub is back with my lemonade."

Nick purposefully danced her away from that side of the dance floor. Hub could wait.

"I hope you won't think I was eavesdropping," she

began, "but I overheard your discussion about your ranch and a loan."

"Yeah, it would move things along a little faster, but I'm not too keen on the debt. Besides, the paperwork is complicated. I've got things to learn."

"Like?"

"I don't think I'm a bad risk. How do I show it on paper? The ranch will produce, but I'd have to make sure I borrow as little capital as I can get by with, but not so little I can't do what needs doing."

"You're not a *bad risk*. And you arrived at this summation, how?"

"Because I know I'm not." He shrugged. "Some of the other ranchers, they were trying to tell me how to figure things like Return on Investment. And then tips for writing up a wordy business plan. That just seems foolish. I can do it in two words: sell cattle."

"The bank will want specifics. The base herd you'll start with and your expected yield, and how many years out. Estimated expenses, return on the investment—"

"How do you know all that?"

They both froze. "I—I...would give anything to know, but it's a memory." She squeezed her eyes shut tight. "I see flashes of...a ledger. Columns of numbers. Hands turning the pages. And a huge pasture. Horses everywhere. Mountains in the background." She opened her eyes. "Mountains in the background. What if I'm from somewhere nearby?"

He couldn't stop the sag in his spirit that surely showed on his face. "Then someone will find you... soon."

EVEN BEFORE SAM came to stand beside her, Sally knew he had entered the building. Conversations halted abruptly and the cessation of chatter moved like a wave through the crowd on the edge of the dance floor. Men and women tried to stare without being obvious. Sally frowned. There was only one reason he could be here.

"My, how my presence puts a damper on things," he said, hooking his thumbs in his vest pocket.

"This is a gathering of church and respectable folks, Sam," she said without looking at him. "You know you shock them."

He chuckled. "Yes, I do." He was amused by their distress, she knew, but then his face hardened as he scanned the townsfolk standing near them. The men looked away, found other things of interest. "Would you like me to tell you how many of these *respectable* men use my back door to enter Lilith's?"

"All have sinned and come short of the glory of God," she quoted. "I have no delusions about anyone in this town."

"Except me."

Her turn to chuckle. "You are the one I don't give up on. That is certainly true."

He sighed, watched the dancers for a moment. Around them, men began to speak softly again, but they watched him, as if he were a lion that might attack any second. *Apropos*, she thought.

"I did have a reason for coming here tonight." He cleared his throat and brushed his green silk cravat down. "I came to ask you if you might dance with me once."

Sally wilted a little. The rumors were already so rampant about Burning Dress. If she danced with Sam in public, everyone would think her girls and his were associated. Nothing could be further from the truth. Sally prayed for the opportunity to rescue *his* girls. Oh, how could she continue to have such a soft spot for a man like him?

"Is that a no?"

On the other hand, white-hot fear of Sam kept the town in line. He was the unofficial protector of her and the ranch. And he'd killed once for her.

"Everyone wonders about us, our past history, Sally. Let's give them something else to talk about. Besides, gossip all they want, everyone knows you are the best representation of Jesus in Hell's Half-Acre."

"And I should avoid appearances of evil." She turned to him. "Dancing with you wouldn't reflect just on me. It's the girls."

She saw the hurt in his dark eyes, but he masked it quickly. "Yes, of course. I understand. Some other time, perhaps, away from prying eyes."

He nodded and left, since he had no reason to hang about, she thought. He had no friends in this room. Except her, and she had to be careful with perceptions.

Someday, Lord, that prodigal is coming home. I won't stop praying till he does.

CHAPTER FOURTEEN

"TRULY ALARMING THE WAY SHE JUST VANISHED." HARVEY Fenton took a sip of his champagne and regarded Kevin with, no doubt, sincere compassion.

Fenton is a good man, Kevin thought with disdain. "Thank you, but we have multiple detectives on the case. Her father is going to start running national advertisements. We'll find her."

Two lovely young ladies in tailored silk gowns coyly cut between the men and batted their eyelashes as they did. Kevin and Harvey nodded politely but continued with their discussion.

"I'm sure you will," Harvey said. "Nonetheless, how disturbing. She seemed fine when last I saw her." He frowned, as if that wasn't totally accurate.

Kevin plucked a glass of bubbly from a passing waiter and tilted his head at Harvey. "You don't seem so sure."

He shook off the concern. "Nothing to do with her disappearance. I came to evaluate Shebar. As you know, I was going to purchase him, but I had…an advisor with me who suggested I buy sturdier horses."

Kevin found this news intriguing. He remembered Sierra had been quite agitated at dinner and had mentioned Harvey had backed out of the sale. The advisor was a new piece of information. "Tell me about him."

Harvey chuckled and shoved his free hand into his pocket. "My favorite bartender's brother. A cowboy from a large ranch somewhere. Antonio said no one knows horses like his brother, Nick. He was in town and, it turned out, more than happy to assess Shebar with me."

"But you didn't buy him."

"No, I did not, and Miss Caldwell was fit to be tied. Nick, however, did me a favor in the long run. I was letting her beauty lead me around like a puppy."

"Has anyone questioned this cowboy about her disappearance?"

Harvey's eyes widened with surprise. "Surely you don't think he had—"

"I don't know what to think. She's missing. No one has sent ransom notes." Either she didn't want to be found or someone… "What if…what if Sierra confronted the man again later? And he…harmed her." God forbid. Without Sierra, he could kiss Mr. Caldwell's support goodbye.

"He truly didn't seem that upset…though…"

"What?"

"Well, he did seem astonished that I was willing to pay ten thousand dollars for the horse. Perhaps he… could he have…?"

"Estimated her wealth. Hatched a plot to kidnap her and hasn't come forth with his demands yet?" Or, the plot had gone awry and Sierra was…if she were gone, as in dead, perhaps that would engender Mr. Caldwell's eternal support for a grieving *almost*-son-in-law. That was a new thought, and Kevin liked it. "Harvey, I think this man must be questioned. How do we find him?"

"Oh." He exhaled. "I can barely recall. Something about a dress. Flames." He waved his hand, as if erasing a chalkboard. "I'll go see Antonio tomorrow. He'll tell me how to find his brother."

NICK WHISTLED and waved his rope at the yearling in front of him. "Quit trying to wander off, you."

Beside him, Sarah chuckled. "She wants to do anything but go back to the herd."

"Well, I've got news for her, that's exactly where she's going."

Ever since the dance, something had changed between Nick and Sarah. They were friendlier to each other. Which made the lie he was carrying around even more of a burden. He was going to have to come clean. He wanted to, but the second she knew who she was, she would shoot straight back to that father of hers.

It occurred to him that he wasn't too thrilled with the idea of her leaving. But she sure as heck wouldn't stay. Not when she remembered the cowboy who had fouled up her high-dollar horse sale. Frustrated, he slapped the rope at the ornery heifer.

"Are you all right?" she asked.

"Fine."

She chewed on her lip a second and then took her gaze back out to the sweeping hills alive with swaying, emerald grass. She shrugged a shoulder as if to say *fine, I won't ask again.*

What if she knows absolutely nothing about her father's business?

No, based on what she knew about ranching, she had to. The notion depressed and angered him. *Then again,* he countered, *maybe she wasn't the one who made the deals.* That was likely a man's business, and she might *not* know the details.

He sighed, aggravated with his seesawing brain. He could tell her, or the detective would tell her eventually. Either one of them could be responsible for her memories coming back. And when they did, she was going to remember Nick. And wonder what kind of game he'd been playing.

What had he been thinking? How had he gotten himself into this?

"Sarah, I've got to tell—"

"Oh, no, look," she said, standing up in the saddle and pointing.

A calf had gotten itself mired in one of the mud wallows on the edge of the creek and was bellowing like he was dying. She was off like a shot to rescue the critter. Nick sighed in defeat and raced after her, aware they had time. Both for the lie to come out and to save the calf.

But not a lot.

The animal was almost unrecognizable, he was so coated in thick, heavy mud, but he was kicking and crying with plenty of strength. "Here"—Nick leaped from the saddle and tossed one end of his reins to Sarah—"hold this."

Not looking forward to the mess this always made of his boots, he strode into the muck. "All right, little fella." The animal kicked helplessly and bawled as Nick tried to get his arms under him. Mud seeped into his boots, then his gloves. He grunted and strained trying to free up the calf. The mud made a sucking sound and he felt the two of them sink a little deeper. He was wet now from his chest down. "Come on, come on, get your feet underneath ya."

Sarah jumped from her horse and waded into the mud. "Here, I can help." Their eyes met over the calf's back. "It's only mud."

"True." They both pushed, shoved, tugged, grunted, and groaned, and in a couple of minutes, the animal broke free of the muck, scrambled up the bank, and trotted off to find his mother. Winded, sweaty, mud-encrusted, Nick dropped to his knees. It was going to be a miserable ride back. He had the mess up his nose and down his pants, and every place in between.

He glanced over at Sarah and literally had to look again. She was covered in mud up to her chest. The bottom of her blonde braid was caked with it. Muck streaked her face and dotted her nose. He couldn't help but laugh. "You're filthy."

"Oh, am I?" She picked up a handful of mud and wiped it down his cheek. "You missed a spot." Apparently, his shocked expression tickled her and she burst out laughing.

Not to be outdone, Nick grabbed his own handful of mud and intended to slather her face up good, but she resisted, grabbing his hand. He persisted and somehow, laughing and wrestling, they wound up on the ground, he on top of her. They both froze, their gazes locked on each other.

She was the most adorable mud pie he'd ever seen.

And he wanted to kiss her, muck and all.

He drifted toward her, as if drawn by some irresistible force. She didn't move. She didn't try to stop him. Her mouth parted ever-so-slightly.

An alarm bell went off in Nick's head and he pulled back, swallowing his shock and fear. "It's getting late." He clambered to his feet and gave her a hand up, trying to ignore the shock—and maybe disappointment—on her face. "Yeah, uh, we'd, uh, better head back," he repeated. "Take half the water at the ranch to clean us up."

"Yeah. And then some."

He almost let her gaze hold him still once more, but with sheer force of will, he strode past her to his horse.

A GOOD SCRUB and Sarah felt like a new person. Towel draped over her head, she sat down at the vanity the girls shared and slowly began drying her hair. Staring at her reflection, she saw again the look in Nick's eyes. She was convinced he'd almost kissed her. And she'd wanted him to.

What had stopped him?

Was it a good thing he had?

Of course it was. She couldn't get involved with him. She didn't know who she was. What if she were married? The thought caused her pulse to triple. Wondering about a husband before had been almost academic. Now, with this…this… "Attraction," she whispered. *I could be on the verge of adultery.*

She shook off the thought. *No, that's ridiculous.* She glanced at her left hand. "I'm not married." This she was sure of. "Fiancé, then?" The thought evoked an unpleasant feeling, a dread—

"Talking to yourself?"

Sarah looked at April in the mirror. "No. Yes. I guess I was."

The girl laughed and sat down on her bunk a few feet away and started pulling off her boots. "Are you thinking about Nick?"

"What makes you ask that?"

"The way he was looking at you at the dance the other night. And the way you were looking at him this morning as you rode out."

Sarah thought about arguing but went back to drying her hair instead. "I think he almost kissed me today."

April gasped. "Almost? What stopped him?"

Sarah frowned. That was a good question. "I don't know. Maybe the fact that I have no memory of who I am."

"Oh. You could have a husband, you mean?"

"No. I don't. I know I don't. I just...know."

"Then what stops you from going to see him this evening and...poke the fire?"

Sarah gasped this time. "I would never be so forward."

"You don't have to be forward. You just need an excuse." The girl laughed, her accent making the suggestion sound so sweet and harmless. "I bet if we put our heads together, we could come up with something."

Sarah's hands stilled. "I think I could help him with his loan paperwork."

April grimaced. "Not very exciting. I was thinking you could take to the bunkhouse one of Maude's pies, but paperwork is good, too."

SALLY'S ROOM was the only one with a balcony. On the west end of the huge log home, it afforded a perfect view of the barn, the outbuildings, the corral, and most of the section they called The Red Hills, so named for the summer mist that often accumulated on them and turned red with the rising sun.

Dusk on a summer evening often drew her here to read scripture and contemplate the day, and pray over her charges, their progress…or lack thereof. *I've been pushing Nick at Sarah, Lord. Something has to give. His conscience or her memory. For his sake, I hope it's his conscience.*

As if signaling He'd heard and was working on the problem, Sarah appeared from under the eaves of the house, striding to the bunkhouse with a yellow notepad tucked beneath her arm.

Curious, Sally rose and stepped over to the log rail. Sarah spoke to the cowboy sitting on the porch, who reached back and hammered on the bunkhouse door. A moment later, Nick appeared, a dishcloth in his hands.

After a short conversation, he tossed the cloth into the lap of his comrade and joined Sarah. The pair headed back toward the big house.

Sally smiled and winked at heaven.

CHAPTER FIFTEEN

NICK ROSE AND STRETCHED, AND THEN STEPPED OVER AND tossed a small log on the fire. The library was picking up a chill. He knew this because Sarah, hunched over the legal pad, had rubbed her arms twice now.

She looked up at him and grinned. "Thank you. I was getting cold."

"I could tell." He rolled his shoulders and drifted to a shelf to eyeball a row of books. "This business plan stuff. Mighty boring."

"Yes, I suppose, but it's important to the bank. They want to see your goals for your ranch and how you've arrived at them." She glanced at the paper covered in her handwriting and several lines of numbers. "It makes you look like you know what you're doing."

"I do know what I'm doing." He turned around and dropped his hands on his hips. "All those numbers we've written down. I can see that in my head. Everybody knows, for example, calf crop percentage is seventy to ninety-five percent. The heritability of calving interval or fertility is only around ten percent. So the variation in calving is impacted by feeding, grass management, and herd health."

Her brow arched as if she were impressed. "My, it's impressive what you know up here," she said as she tapped her forehead, "but"—she tapped the notepad—"we have to show the bank your formulas."

He sighed and came back to the table. "Okay." He sat down again and couldn't help but take a moment to study her face. Such pretty, smooth cheeks, long eyelashes that framed inviting jade eyes. He'd pay five dollars to see her take that braid out again and let all that shimmering, red-blonde hair loose.

"Nick, are you listening to me?"

"What? Nope. Sorry. I was thinking about…range management."

"Good. Let's write a few thoughts about that. How big is your spread?"

"Six hundred acres."

"All right." She started writing. "And you've already said you want your initial herd size to float around one hundred and fifty head—"

Nick reached out and touched her hand, stopping the pencil. She looked up, startled.

"Thank you. I appreciate you helping me with this. I really do."

She blushed and went back to the paper. "I don't mind. I hope it will jog something loose in my stubborn brain."

"Just the same. Thanks." The more she helped him, the worse he felt about things. *Yeah, this has to stop. Time to come clean and let the chips fall—*

The library door opened slowly and Maude, the busty, older, gray-haired woman who ran the kitchen, let herself in carrying a tray of coffee service.

"Oh, hey." Nick leaped to his feet and stepped over to take the load. "Let me."

"Miss Sally suggested you would appreciate some coffee and the fritters. Enjoy. And don't work too late, you two."

"We won't. Thank you." Nick set down the tray and then returned to close the door all the way. After all, they needed to keep the heat in the library.

Sarah was already pouring the coffee when he came back to the table.

"How did she know we were in here?" Nick asked, mildly curious.

Sarah's hands slowed. "I think Miss Sally knows a lot of things…"

He took his seat again, now more curious. "What do you mean?"

"Haven't you ever noticed anything…unusual about her?"

He immediately thought of that day she'd questioned him about his activities in Denver. As if she'd already known the answers. And the cat. The way Little Joe had acted…almost human around her. "Not really," he said, choosing to ignore the things he didn't understand.

Sarah tapped her pencil on the paper and shook her head. "I could have sworn one time I saw—" She dismissed the thought with a nervous laugh. "Never mind."

"What?"

"You'll think I'm crazy."

"Doesn't matter what I think."

"True. And I know what I saw. The lightning bugs were…listening to her."

Nick took a second to let her meaning sink in. It didn't. "I don't follow."

"They were flitting around her one evening, and she seemed to—to command them. Then she told them to go away, and they dispersed. Like they understood every word she said. *Bugs*."

"Like Little Joe," he said, remembering the poor manners of the cat.

"Pardon?"

"Her cat."

"Oh."

"She talks to him like he's human, and he goes off and does whatever she says. Mind you, I'm talking about a cat."

They both sat in silence for a moment, pondering, he supposed, the mysterious Miss Sally. "I reckon it's stuff like that that keeps the rumors about this place going, so don't repeat what you saw."

Sarah pulled away from the table. "Rumors?"

"Yeah, there's a few folks in town that throw some pretty slanderous gossip around. A ranch with mostly women running it, and it's one of the finest operations in Colorado."

"Doesn't sit right with the men?"

"A lot of them, no. The smart ones leave her and her ranch alone. There are a couple who whisper things. I tell you, though, there's a fella in town who'll pinch your head off if he hears you."

"That's interesting. She has a knight in shining armor?"

Nick almost shivered. "Sam Hain's a lot of things, but that ain't one of 'em. If anything, he's the Black Knight."

Sarah frowned as if she couldn't put all this information together. Nick leaned in, gave her a firm look. "Nobody knows their history. They were the first white folks in the valley. They go way back, and that's all Miss Sally will say. You don't ask Sam Hain unless you want a gun barrel in your mouth. It's a real sore subject with him."

"Well, unless he's sitting on the board at the bank, we don't need to worry about him. Let's get this finished so you can get *your* ranch running."

"YOU REALLY DIDN'T HAVE to tag along," Harvey said, pushing open the door to the Red Door Gentleman's Club.

Kevin followed, annoyed with the man's attitude. "You act as if this saloon of yours is some great secret."

"It's not that."

Kevin surveyed the public house, a dark, dreary affair. The few patrons here for a liquid dinner looked up, surveyed his and Harvey's tailored suits, but went back to their drinks without any reaction.

"Good Lord, this place is..."

"Rough. I know. That's the reason I like it. No one bothers me here. I needn't put on airs and talk about the banking business till I want to choke on the subject. I can have a drink in peace."

Kevin agreed there was something to be said for the argument.

Harvey strode up to the bar and greeted the bartender with an almost relieved tone in his voice. "Antonio, it's good to see you."

"Mr. Fenton." Antonio, a big man in his thirties, with dark hair and dark eyes, tossed his towel over his shoulder and joined them. "Good to see you."

"You, too. This is my friend, Kevin Hartman." The

two nodded at each other. "Set us up with two shots, if you would, and I'd like to ask about your brother."

The barkeep retrieved a bottle of whiskey from beneath the bar, set up two snifters, and poured. "Ask away." He slid the glasses to each of them.

"Is he back at the ranch or is he still in town?"

"No, Nick was only here for a quick visit. Left the day he looked at those horses with ya. You need some more horse advice or horses?"

"Horses. He mentioned the ranch he works for sells them. I thought I'd go take a look, but I couldn't remember—

"Burning Something Ranch. About a hundred or so miles out from here. Near a little crossroads that ain't on the map. Place called Hell's Half-Acre."

Harvey chuckled. "Interesting name for a town—"

"A hundred miles," Kevin interrupted. "In what direction?"

Antonio blinked. "You know, I never asked. I don't know."

Anger ignited instantly in Kevin, and he wanted to smash a bottle over the fool's head. This *was* helpful information, but the idiot's lack of detail was also an annoying delay. He tossed back his drink and spared a glare for Harvey. "Thank you. Enjoy your drink."

As he stormed from the low-class establishment, he heard Harvey apologizing for him. "You have to overlook him, Tony. His lady friend has gone missing and he's worried."

While Kevin had no idea where Hell's Half-Acre was, he was sure Devonshire would enlighten him eventually. Therefore, it was a necessity to get Sean's man there before the detective. Kevin had no illusions. Devonshire had the reputation of a bloodhound and would certainly ferret out this morsel of information.

Kevin needed to make sure the situation in the town was nothing that would be detrimental to his own plans. If it was, he needed to have a response in place.

He tapped his hat lower and strode with determination to Sean's grubby little office in the warehouse district.

CHAPTER SIXTEEN

SALLY SPOTTED SAM CROSSING THE STREET IN THE HIGH noon heat and made a beeline for him. If the man didn't stop selling inferior barbed wire she was going to string him up with—

She stopped in the shadow of the bakery's porch and watched as he and another man shook hands in front of the café. They chatted for a moment, doing introductions, she assumed. Sam spotted her just then and subtly waved her off. Heeding his surreptitious signal, she took a step backward then spun and headed for the bench in front of the mercantile.

From her vantage point, she could see the two of them talking but not hear them.

Who is this man, Father? Nearly as tall as Sam, but scruffy and weathered, he looked like more of the rabble Sam entertained in his saloon. His head was up at a rather cocky angle, and Sally knew that attitude wouldn't last long. Clearly, the man didn't know to whom he was speaking.

So, why did Sam wave her off?

The stranger did most of the talking, motioning pointedly with his hands. Sam listened, nodding now and again…but after a moment, he leaned in a little, and the stranger took a quick step back. His movements stopped. As he stared at Sam, he withered under a dark look, his body shrinking as he hunched up, like a dog tucking its tail between its legs. Abruptly, the man turned and crossed the road, headed toward the stage station, casting a fleeting, fearful glance over his shoulder. Sam waited for the stranger to turn the corner, then ambled down to Sally.

"May I sit?"

She motioned to the far end of the bench and he obliged. "What was that all about?"

"I hope I did not overstep, but he was a, oh, let's say, a rough sort. He was sent here by someone named Kevin Hartman. The name ring a bell?"

"No."

Sam reached into his pocket, withdrew a cigar, and went through the motions of lighting it. "Hartman is looking for his fiancée, a young lady who went missing from Denver a little over a month ago." He tossed away his match.

Sarah? "And?"

"I think he's looking for your little amnesiac."

"Why are you concerned you overstepped?"

"I sent the lowlife on his way and told him not to come back. He is not to give this Mr. Hartman any report about my town or anyone in it."

"Oh." Sally couldn't decide at the moment if that was a good thing or a bad thing. "Looked like you threw the fear of God into him."

"Oh, I threw fear in him all right." His gaze frosted over for a moment. "He won't sleep for a week." He blinked and came back to her. "The man is only a day or two ahead of a detective, also hired by this Hartman."

"Why would he…?" This was all so confusing.

"I assume he wanted to know about conditions on the ground before the detective arrived."

"Why? None of this makes any sense." Sally drummed her fingers, frustrated over the confusing actions by this Hartman fellow. "I canceled the detective you found for me. I have this feeling Nick and Sarah are to work this out on their own."

Sam shrugged and waved the cigar dismissively. "They don't have much time to untangle things." He stood and waved his cheroot in goodbye. "I need a drink." Without a look back, he sauntered off toward the saloon.

———

SALLY CLOSED her Bible and waited. *They don't have much time to untangle things.* Sam's warning was somber and prophetic, she thought. But she did appreciate the time he had bought Nick and Sarah. Speaking of— He knocked on her door. "Come in, Nick."

There was a pause and Sally smiled, but then the door opened and her ranch hand slipped in. "Mornin', Miss Sally."

"Morning."

He waved his hat at the door. "How did you know—uh, never mind." He pressed his Stetson to his chest and cleared his throat. "You have a minute?"

She motioned to the seat in front of her desk and he settled in. She knew part of what he was going to say, but wasn't clear on the other.

"I have an appointment at the bank this morning. I'm going to apply for a loan."

She tilted her head. "I see you have mixed emotions about it."

"I do. Considering the way it worked out for Pa, it's a little unnerving, but with you on the board, and a little advice from the other ranchers, and a good business plan—"

"That Sarah helped you write."

"Yes, ma'am. She did, and I have a lot of confidence it's a good plan."

"As do I. But I have to ask you, Nick, have you prayed about this next step?"

He took a moment to answer. "Yes, ma'am. I think I'm doing the right thing, it's just…just that, well, if you have something in your life…" He tugged on his ear. "Something like a sin, you reckon that hinders the Lord from answering your prayers?"

"If sin hindered our prayers, the Father would never answer any of us," she said lightly. The joke, however, only earned her a pained look. She tried again. "Sin can hinder things, certainly. I suppose it depends on the sin, what you're praying for, and what the Lord's will is in a certain situation."

"Hmm," he grunted.

"Anything you want to get off your chest?"

"Hmm," he grunted once more. Finally, he nodded. "Yes, ma'am, I do. Only, I don't have time just now. I would like to ask your advice on something later. I've dug myself a hole and…"

"First, stop digging."

"Yes, ma'am." He sighed and stood up. "I've got to get to the bank."

"I'll be praying for your approval."

"Miss Sally, thank you. Thank you for everything I've learned here, and thank you for not minding that I want my own place back."

"We don't do this alone, Nick." She rose and offered her hand across her desk. When he took it, she said, "You're going to be a fine, prosperous rancher. It will be my honor to have you as a neighbor."

NICK WALKED out of the bank and stopped like he'd met a brick wall. The conversation with Tyler Gilbert was still ringing in his ears.

And the words were magical.

He'd been approved. The business plan was insightful and conservative. He had money in his bank account. Enough to start his ranch.

And it probably wouldn't have happened if not for Sierra Caldwell.

Nick exhaled heavily and hung his head. The one dark spot on this beautiful day. He rubbed his neck and made up his mind. She had to know. Today.

The peddler's wagon rolled by at that moment, and an idea to soften the blow occurred to Nick.

SARAH FELL BACK across her bed and winced at the dust that rose from her body. Well, she'd take a bath then shake out the blanket…if she could find the strength. She was exhausted, and her rear end felt as if she'd been sitting on a rock all day. How much longer before she was used to being in the saddle sunup to sundown?

Still and all, she liked the exhaustion in a macabre

kind of way. She felt useful. Did she have this feeling in her old life and that was why she liked it? Or did she lack it, and *that* was why she liked it?

"Sarah?"

April's voice. Sarah didn't open her eyes. "Present."

April chuckled, and the rustle of fabric told Sarah she'd moved closer. "Here. I have a note for you. From Nick."

She opened her eyes and saw the piece of paper the girl was holding out to her. A little more energized, she sat up.

"He's downstairs waiting for an answer."

Curious, Sarah took the note and unfolded it. *Dear Sarah, I have some news, and I'd like you to be the first person I share it with. Picnic at my homestead now?*

"Now? He can't even give a girl time to bathe?" Butterflies launched in Sarah's stomach and swirled about as if they were in a hurricane. "I bet he got the loan." She rose and tugged playfully on one of April's red braids. "Could you tell him I'll be down in ten minutes?"

CHAPTER SEVENTEEN

"EITHER WAY THINGS WENT, MISS SALLY, I WAS GOING TO tell her." Nick couldn't even look at his boss. He was pretty ashamed of himself, and getting the loan had just made the burden that much worse.

I shouldn't have waited at all.

"Why did you?"

He rounded on her. Had he said that out loud? "I was just going to have a little fun with her. One day, to let her see how a real working hand lives. Then I found out she's Caldwell's daughter, and my slight offense changed over to wanting a little revenge. But whatever her pa did, I doubt she was any part of it."

Miss Sally was leaning on the edge of her desk. Nodding, she rose and drifted around behind it to sit. She looked pleased. "I don't know how she'll react, and no, you shouldn't have waited, but it's time to move past this. I'll wire her father, phrase things as delicately as possible, try to keep your name out of it. But I won't lie to protect you."

"No, ma'am, I wouldn't ask you to."

"You didn't keep her here against her will exactly, but her father has probably been worried half to death."

Nick hung his head in shame. He'd never even considered that.

"So, I doubt there will be any kind of charges, but I don't think there will be lots of warm feelings."

"You don't think she'll forgive me?"

"You want her to?"

In the worst way. "Yes, ma'am, I do."

"I think being here has been good for our little debutante, Nick. Maybe she'll see that and overlook the rest."

NICK WAITED for Sarah outside in the wagon. A few minutes later, she emerged from the house, a real bounce in her step. It gave him hope.

"We're taking the wagon?" she asked.

"Couldn't get everything I need in the saddlebags. Like him." He motioned to the back. Regarding him with a curious expression, she looked over the side and gasped. Joy lit her face like candles on a Christmas tree. The little, black-and-white speckled puppy leaped up on the rail and licked her straight in the face. Squealing with delight, Sarah stood on her tiptoes and pulled the furry bundle out of the wagon.

"Oh, he's precious! Just precious," she said, dodging his sloppy kisses and laughing.

Nick grinned from ear to ear, for the moment just enjoying her glee with the animal. "I saw you looking at them when the peddler was here. He's a little older—"

"Oh, but no less darling."

Nick scooted over and offered his hand to Sarah. "He can ride up front with us."

Sarah climbed up and settled with the pup in her lap, teasing him with her fingers and growling playfully. "What are you going to name him?"

"Haven't decided." Nick slapped the reins. "Thought you could help me with that."

As they rolled off from the ranch, Sarah cut her eyes at Nick. "A man gets a dog. That says something."

"Something like? And how would you know? Remember something?"

He'd spoken in jest, but her face clouded. "I-I don't know. I say things sometimes that come from...my past. It's like I *feel* them more than I remember them." She shrugged off the dark thoughts. "But never mind. I think I know someone who got a loan today."

He couldn't stop the smile that broke and opened him up clear down to his soul. "One I'm comfortable with. I mean, good, fair terms."

THE AFTERNOON WAS TOO PRETTY to eat in the cabin, so Nick spread a blanket in the grass in the front yard and helped unload the basket of chicken and biscuits. Sarah grabbed the pie and the puppy. "Can I set him down, or do you think he'll run off?"

He set the basket on the blanket and turned back for the pie. "How about I handle the food and you keep an eye on Trouble there?"

She handed off the dessert and lifted the puppy up to eye level. "Twouble? You're not going to be any twouble."

Nick chuckled at the silly little voice she was using. He spread the food out while she used an old bandana to play tug with the pup. "Yeah, I don't think I want to call him Trouble. That sets a bad row. You have any suggestions?"

"Hmmm." She tugged and let the puppy pull the rag in her hand with some fierce growling. "How about... Shebar."

Nick's hand froze and he felt like a mule had kicked him. Slowly, licking his dry lips, he set the chicken in his hand down on a plate and looked up at her. He was sure the name had been her way of saying her memory was back. She'd been toying with him.

But she was only smiling expectantly. "You don't like it?"

"No, I...you just...kind of an odd name."

"I know. It just popped into my head. It's unusual." She growled playfully at Shebar.

Nick winced. He just wanted to enjoy the picnic for a few minutes, and then he was going to tell her. He was dragging his feet, though, and fully accepted his cowardice.

It took some doing to teach the energetic shepherd that the food on the plates was not for him, but eventually he got the message and curled up next to Sarah for a snooze.

With a chicken wing in his hand, Nick waved at the dog. "He likes you."

Sarah reached down and gently rubbed his head. "He's precious." She glanced around the yard and at the cabin. "You're so lucky. I'd love to have all this land to run horses and cattle on."

Another knife in his heart. This couldn't go on much longer. Even if he didn't confess, he was sure Sarah was giving way to Sierra Caldwell. His mood soured as the sun sank lower and lower in the western sky. He always had loved the view from his yard. He could see the edge of Burning Dress land to the east and endless possibilities to the west. Gently rolling green hills and haunting rock formations, painted in the vibrant colors of a fading day, always put him in awe of God's handiwork.

"It's getting late."

He blinked and looked at her. She was staring back at him with a puzzled, maybe curious, glint in her eyes.

"But I feel like there's something on your mind. You want to talk about it?"

No. He absolutely did not want to, and he wished for the millionth time he'd never gotten himself into this mess. "Yeah, but I'd like to wait a bit longer. Enjoy the sunset ride back to the ranch."

"Fine by me."

But he saw the troubled crease come to her brow.

CHAPTER EIGHTEEN

Sally sensed Sam was coming before he drove his surrey over the hill. She wasn't surprised he had guests. Two men she didn't know, but she suspected who they were. She dropped the lace curtain on her window and huffed. "Well, Father, I pray this goes well. I pray Sierra finds her answers and that Nick finds peace."

With the certainty that this play was coming to an end, she walked outside and met them as they rolled in. "Sam. Gentlemen."

Sam, grim-faced, locked the brake and jumped down from the buggy, simultaneously pulling his hat off. "Sally, these men are looking for someone."

He might as well have said the girl's name. He knew very well who these men were. She wasn't sure how she felt about him bringing them here. A little betrayed?

She turned her gaze to the two well-dressed lawyer-types, wearing expensive suits and glistening shoes. As they climbed down, their ages and relationship became apparent. The young man with cleanly cut, wavy blond hair was the know-it-all type, pretending to serve the other man, while secretly belittling him. The older man was in his fifties, commanding, but wearied by his recent stress.

Of course, Sally knew who they were immediately, and she shot a disapproving glare at Sam. He shrugged, noncommittally. "They were coming with me or without me. I thought it might be helpful if I were here."

She didn't argue, but turned to the men, her hand extended. "I'm Miss Sally. Welcome to Burning Dress Ranch."

The older man spoke first. "Jason Caldwell." He inclined his head. "I believe we've met before."

"Once. Years ago. You wanted my banking business."

"I remember. You were one of the hold-outs."

"Fortunately."

Caldwell scowled and the other man interjected himself before the conversation worsened. "Kevin Hartman. We're looking for Miss Sierra Caldwell. Mr. Caldwell's daughter and my fiancée."

Sally raised her brow at the lie, but the silhouette of a wagon emerging on the ridge made her objections moot. "Those two might know something."

The men tracked her gaze and waited.

THE SUN SET COMPLETELY behind the distant mountains, and Sarah hugged Shebar a little tighter as protection from the sudden chill. Beside her, Nick had gone decidedly sullen, his eyes glued to the ranch house falling into shadows…and the guests standing out front.

Sarah tilted her head. Something about their shapes was familiar.

Deciding she'd rather tease the puppy, she wagged a

finger in his face. "Shebar, get it," she whispered in a teasing tone. "Get it."

The puppy yapped and snapped at her finger.

Nick pulled the wagon up beside the surrey and yanked the brake.

"I'll take Shebar and put him in the barn," Sarah said, moving to climb down. "I bet Maude has some scraps for him." She reached the ground, careful of the pup, and glanced at the men. "Father, Kevin. Give me a moment." She strode quickly to the barn, intent on securing Shebar in a stall. Out of the corner of her eye, she saw Hub join the group, a sheepish grin on his face.

NICK'S HEART fell clear to his toes. She'd said their names. She knew them.

No one breathed.

No one moved.

Then, as she disappeared into the shadowy barn, Hub sidled up to Caldwell and the younger fella. "Looks like I was able to help you fellows out, after all."

"You did indeed help us narrow down the ranch," Caldwell said, eyeing Nick with suspicion. "If I find that my daughter has been kept here against her will—"

"Which I think is highly likely," Kevin interjected angrily.

"If she has, I'll bring the full force and weight of the Colorado State—"

"Hub," Miss Sally said coolly, stopping the men and their threats. "What did you do?"

Suddenly, he shrank a little lower, like a coyote caught in the hen house. "I knew something was up when Nick saw Miss Sarah at the train station. And then, a few days ago, I saw a paper from Denver with her picture in it. So, I let her pa know I thought she was here. There was a big reward."

"Father?"

All eyes rocketed to Sarah, standing in the barn entrance, Shebar still in her arms. Nick held his breath.

"Kevin?" For a moment, she looked confused, but Nick could see the flood of memories piling up, the dam bursting, the confusion giving way to...betrayal.

Her gaze slid to him. Even in the low light, he registered her disappointment and felt the heat of it.

Her gaze flicked to Hub and she sneered at him, but she came right back to Nick. "You've both been hiding the truth from me. He's just a petty opportunist, but you —" her voice broke and she stopped. "You knew the truth all along. You tricked me. And you mocked me." Her voice dropped. "Then you used me." Her lips tightened into a thin, angry line. "You've got your loan. You've got your ranch. I hope you choke on it."

Nick felt about two inches tall. He felt lower than Shebar's belly, so he just sat there in the wagon and took it. Because he deserved every word of the abuse. "For what it's worth, Sierra, I was just trying to get back at your father. Doesn't make it right. Not at all, but it's an explanation."

"I'm so glad I could be of use. Just what did my father do?"

"When he first brought his bank to town, he helped a lot of ranchers and farmers refinance their land, but steep monthly payments were part of the deal. My pa lost everything because of his bank." He glared at Caldwell. "He shot himself down by the pond."

Sierra flinched. "I'm sorry, but that didn't give you the right—"

"I know." He shrugged his shoulders feebly. "I know. And I'm sorry."

"Yes. Yes, you are." Sierra walked over to Miss Sally, still holding the puppy. "Thank you. I learned that there are things in me that run deeper than how I was raised or how I should act."

Miss Sally reached out and squeezed her shoulder. "Come back any time, Sierra."

"We will press charges," Kevin threatened, glaring at Nick.

"No," Sierra said firmly, turning away from Miss Sally. "We're leaving. Now." She started to move but realized she still had the puppy in her arms. Sniffling, she set him on the ground. For a moment, she stared into his sweet, curious face, tongue hanging out with excitement. "Take care, Shebar."

NICK STOOD SILENTLY, hopelessly, as Sierra marched to the surrey, climbed in, and stared stoically into the distance. Caldwell and Kevin had exchanged awkward glances, then piled in with her. Hain cast an apologetic glance to Miss Sally, took the driver's seat, and drove them away.

Nick couldn't remember a time he'd felt so ashamed but boiling with fury, too. Hub had lied and manipulated them and—

And Nick had done exactly the same things.

Without looking at Miss Sally, sick of his own company, more than ready to clock Hub, Nick jumped down from the wagon, swept Shebar into his arms, and strode to the barn.

"I'll be back, boy," he said as he deposited the puppy

into a stall. Shuffling behind him announced company, and he sensed it was Miss Sally. "I'm going to go for a ride," he told her. "I need—"

"Take your time."

She was awfully patient with him, and he appreciated it, but he'd let her down, too…

OUT IN THE middle of the prairie now, not a human in sight, the sky a riot of oranges and reds quickly giving way to the purple of night, he locked the brake and jumped to the ground. The weight of his sin pressing on his soul, he managed two steps before he fell to his knees.

"Oh, God, I'm worthless." He shook his head, sick over the quagmire he'd created. "I'm just a coward. I could have told her." He snorted in disgust. "Told her? I should have never started down this path in the first place. It was just mean-spirited, and I wanted to…hurt someone for what Pa did…"

He collapsed back on his bum. He didn't feel like sobbing. He felt like banging his head against a rock. "I thought I was a better man than this, Lord. Better than my pa—"

He stopped his whining and thought about things for a moment. Failed crops, sick cows, then your wife dies, and you lose your ranch. *That* was a lot for a man to carry. Yet, a little shame, some dirty looks…and a woman he'd come to care about had Nick on his knees like his world was falling apart.

And on his knees was exactly where he should have been all along. *I let a grudge twist me into a man I didn't recognize. Then I closed You out, Lord. Went along my merry way, thinking this joke would sort itself out. Well, it sure has sorted out, all right.* He glanced to the north. To Denver.

To her.

"She hates me. I hate me. I let Miss Sally down." But worse than all of it was how he'd just stuffed God over into a corner, out of sight, out of mind. "I'm sorry, Lord."

A scripture whispered in his mind. *Pride goes before destruction. And a haughty spirit before a fall.*

Yeah, I guess that's about right. Only, I'm not feeling so haughty just now. I'm sorry, Lord. I ask Your forgiveness, and someday, when I can look her in the eye...I'll ask for hers.

CHAPTER NINETEEN

"You're not ready for my top bull." Sally rested her arms on the rail at the corral and savored the warm sun on her shoulders. Her Hereford bull, King George, bellowed as if he agreed and pawed the ground. "He'd be a big investment. Take too much of your operating capital."

Beside her, Nick nodded. "Yes, ma'am. I wouldn't disagree. So why are we standing here talking about him?"

"You came to cut out your herd today. Several of the heifers in the Red Canyon herd are in season. Take six. I'll *loan* you George there for a stud fee, and sell you a different bull at a good price."

Nick's mouth dropped open. "You'd do that for me? Even after what I...what I did?"

"Not your finest moment, but you've asked for forgiveness. He doesn't hold it against you. Neither do I. We both expect you not to repeat such foolishness."

"You don't have to worry about that," he mumbled.

Sally felt for the young man. He looked miserable. "I don't stud George out to just anybody."

"I know. That's why my mouth is hanging open. Thank you."

She looked into the future and smiled. "You're going to be a prosperous rancher, Nick. You've forgiven the wrongs of the past. Now God can work with you. If you'll get out of His way, He'll bless you."

He let out a long, slow breath. "Some days I do feel... kind of on the verge of something breaking my way."

"But...?"

"But, I'm missing something to make it all come together."

Sally drummed her gloved fingers on the rail and watched George lumber over to the water trough. "You know, all Sierra wanted was to be respected. Valued for her brains, not her beauty. Not told what to do, but allowed to think, and have opinions."

"All I did was lie to her and use her to get my loan."

"God designed the woman to stand beside Adam. Not behind him, not in front of him. Sierra will make someone a good partner one day."

He began tugging on his gloves with short, angry moves. "Yeah, I reckon she will. She'll marry some doctor or lawyer and live in a big house and go to political dinners—"

"And hate every minute of it."

He stopped moving. "She's made for more."

Miss Sally allowed a tiny smile to lift one side of her mouth. "Start with the stables."

"I beg your pardon?"

Sally chuckled as she turned and started walking away from the corral. *Sometimes I don't think before I speak, Lord.* "Nothing," she called over her shoulder. "Just thinking out loud. Let's go cut out your herd."

Quite the party *for a last-minute gathering.*

Sierra smiled stiffly at the people patting her on the back or clutching her hand with warm well-wishes. A few people hugged her. No one asked where she'd been, but she could see the curiosity in their eyes.

So many faces she should know under the glowing chandeliers. But she could only see April and her adorable, muscular arms, Melissa swinging a rope over her head and chasing cattle, Maude rolling out the most amazing, delicious biscuits, Gilly laughing and blushing every time Hub came near her. Sierra hoped Polly was happy and doing well on her farm.

Sierra missed the ranch and the women who were more real to her than anyone at this party.

Kevin emerged from the crowd, circled his arm around her waist, and conducted her into the swirling, twirling mass of silk tuxedos and satin ball gowns moving in time with a string quartet. "I thought I told you to wear the violet gown this evening," he said, looking over her head. "Blue is not your best color."

She wondered why he did that. And he did it often. Looking *over* her, rather than *at* her. As if he was more concerned with who saw him with Sierra Caldwell than what she thought about anything. Was she merely a prop? The truth of the idea grated on her nerves the more she considered it.

"Tomorrow," he continued, "I've an important dinner engagement with the attorney general. Your father arranged it. I think it would be nice if you went to some extra trouble with your appearance."

Sierra nearly stopped dancing. She did stumble. Kevin ignored that as well. "What do you mean extra trouble?" she asked.

"I don't know. Whatever it is you women do when you spend all day at the spa. Make your skin glow. Your hair glimmer. Cinch your corset a touch tighter."

Sierra didn't know whether to kick Kevin in the shin or simply stomp off with steam coming from her ears. In the past month, she'd participated in some very rugged and uncouth exercises. She'd fed a filthy hog and wallowed in the mud to save a calf, to name a few. Trying to fit into the delicate, high society mold had never sat well with her. Now, it chafed like a wet, wool shift.

She glanced around the room, full of the wealthiest and finest families in Denver society and beyond. She didn't like any of these people. She missed Burning Dress.

She missed Nick.

But that bridge was in ashes.

Lost in these miserable, dark thoughts, she was only a little surprised when Kevin stepped back and handed her over to her father for a dance. "Good evening, dear," he said, taking her hands.

"Good evening, Father," she tried with some enthusiasm. They had not talked about her time at the ranch, either. It was as if neither he nor Kevin cared, just so long as she was back being the dutiful daughter. The fiancée part of this play simply wasn't going to happen, but she'd cross that bridge when she came to it.

"I thought you were going to wear the emerald gown tonight, the one from House of Worth?" he asked as he coolly spun her around.

She deflated with the tedium of the question. "Kevin made a request, as well."

"So you prefer his opinion over mine? A harbinger of things to come?" Her father raised his eyebrows.

"Hardly. And you misunderstand. Neither of you requested blue. Furthermore, I have no interest whatsoever in a relationship of any kind with Kevin." Surely that was clear.

"That boy has a future. That's all I'll say on the matter." His tone thrummed with a firm warning.

THE FIRST MOMENT she had free, Sierra slipped away from the stodgy party and scurried to the barn. Inhaling the calming scent of alfalfa, horses, and freshly oiled tack, she drifted through the barn, heedless of the dust accumulating on the hem of her very expensive gown.

A dozen stable hands were busy putting the horses away for the evening. They acknowledged her with pleasant but puzzled smiles as they brushed the animals, stuffed their racks with hay, and dumped feed in their buckets. She paused at Cleopatra's stall. Inside, Julio was grooming the palomino and humming softly to her.

An employee of at least a decade, he was a wise-and-weathered older gentleman. He looked up at Sierra and nodded. "Miss Sierra. It is good to see you back. You went away somewhere, *sí*?"

Went away? As good an answer as any. "*Sí*. I was visiting another ranch."

"Oh, was it nice?"

"Yes. Yes it was." But thinking about it made her sad, and she didn't want to be sad. On a whim, and with a devil-may-care attitude, she opened the stall gate and stepped inside. "I'd like to help groom her."

Julio straightened, his eyes wide as he scanned her gown. "I don't know..." he said hesitantly. "The last time—"

"I don't give two figs about Mr. Hartman." She snatched the brush from his hand, then stopped, aware she'd been shockingly rude. "I'm sorry. But I really would like to brush her." It was the only form of rebellion she could conjure at the moment.

Julio shrugged. "Is okay with me. You're the boss." He plucked another brush from a bucket near his feet and moved to the other side of the horse.

"I miss grooming the horses."

"And they miss you. We miss when you were little and you would help."

She looked across Cleopatra's back at the man. "Why did you say it like that? You didn't miss me when I got older? I didn't help as much, but—"

"When you were little, you didn't know you were the boss. When you were a teenager, you started..." he faded off and brushed a little faster.

Now Sierra was curious. "Julio, you've worked for us long enough to know you can say whatever it was you started to say."

He considered things a moment, then shrugged. "When you started getting older, you started acting like a boss around us. But not a good boss. More like the dons from my country." He bobbed his head, as if a little embarrassed, and went back to brushing.

Sierra's hand paused. She hadn't even noticed she'd lost the camaraderie of the stable hands. She'd forgotten the days of drawing straws to see who would spread the manure pile. At ten years old, that had been her most hated job. Somehow, Julio had always lost when it was between him and her.

But at fifteen, the pressure to be socially acceptable to her father and his wife and their new friends had begun to mount. At first, Sierra hadn't minded the restrictions and expectations too much, but then, just in the last year, thanks to Kevin's annoying presence, she began to understand where these social games were taking her: to a land of pointless meetings, shallow friendships, low expectations...and marriage for profit.

"I'm sorry," she whispered, and then said it louder for Julio. "I'm sorry."

He began to braid Cleopatra's mane with quick, expert movements. "It's all right. I do not think you can help it. Much."

CHAPTER TWENTY

LAMENTING THE SELFISH AND CONFINING LIFE SHE'D allowed herself to fall into, Sierra bid Julio good night and drifted down to the end of the barn. To see the reason she was out here.

She'd been putting it off for some reason.

Probably because she knew when she looked at Shebar, she'd see a tall, dark, and handsome cowboy holding a little, black-and-white speckled puppy…in front of a fireplace mantle topped off with wildflowers.

Shaking her head at all the melancholy emotions roiling in her heart, she took the final step and peered into Shebar's stall. The stallion stood in the center, black as a midnight sky, glistening like a still lake beneath a moon. His ears were forward, his head was up, and he was just as stunning as ever.

"Shebar," she whispered. The horse grumbled and hurried over, evidently happy to see his favorite human. "I've missed you, too," she said, patting his head, which he shook and swung and grumbled with excitement. "But I'd still like to sell you. The home could use the money. Just because I'm in a gilded cage is no reason to be useless to humanity."

The sound of a riding crop slicing through the air made her spin. Kevin stepped out of the shadows and slapped the crop across his palm with enough force that Sierra knew it had to hurt him. The heat in his eyes, however, immediately declared his intentions with it.

She moved back from him, but came up against the stall door. *Oh, God, help me...*

She was afraid, but she wasn't frozen in fear

"It's time you had a lesson in obedience, Sierra."

He smacked his hand again, and she saw the welt forming in his palm. She cast about, looking for something to use as a weapon. "Touch me and I'll scream bloody murder."

He laughed and reached for her. At the same instant, Sierra grabbed a coiled rope hanging on a hook and slapped it upside his head. As he knocked it away, she tried to dive past him, but he grabbed the back of her gown and swung her violently back into the stall door, the crop raised for a strike. It came down across the top of her shoulder, burning a trail of fire, and she did scream. He raised the whip again, but she grabbed his hand and sank her nails into his flesh, growling like a mad woman. With his free hand, he slapped her and sent her reeling. An ill-placed bucket tangled her feet, and she slammed hard to the ground.

Stars and fireworks danced before her eyes, but she knew what was coming and tried to block the next strike. This time, the whip landed across her back. The pain was searing. Sierra screamed again, but now fury fueled her voice.

She raised her arm defensively and struggled against the trappings of the gown to gain her feet. The crop slashed across her forearm, scorching her flesh. Somehow, she managed to grab a horseshoe hanging on a hook and lobbed it at Kevin with everything in her. It missed, and he clawed for her hands, wrestling with her like a madman. She gouged, kicked, bellowed, but he pinned her arms behind her back. Turning her away from him, he slashed her again across her shoulders, and she cried out in pain and rage.

And then, suddenly, Kevin went flying across the breezeway into the wall, collapsing in a clatter of pitchforks and shovels. Her arms and shoulders burning from his strikes, Sierra spun and watched in disbelief as Nick grabbed Kevin, snatched him to his feet, and crashed a beefy fist into his face.

Blood gushed from Kevin's nose, but he fought back. "I'll beat her, then I'll beat you, you bumpkin," he raged, delivering a powerful right hook to Nick's jaw.

Nick shook off the blow. "You'll never touch her again," he snarled. Pushing Kevin off him, he loosed a lightning-fast barrage of brutal blows on the lawyer, who staggered back with each one. The final uppercut slowed Kevin, had him swaying. His eyes glazed over. Nick waited, chest heaving, bloodied hands up. Then Kevin fell face-first into the brick.

NICK SPUN and raced to Sierra. "Are you all right?" His hands fanned out over her. He hesitated to touch her. She had welts rising on her arms and shoulders, but then he abruptly swept her into his arms and headed down the breezeway.

Sierra looked thunderstruck. Pain, but joy, too,

cascaded over her face. He tried not to read too much into it.

"What are you doing here?" she asked.

A short, older Mexican man came running into the barn, a lantern in his hand. "Miss Sierra, what is happening?" He glared at Nick.

"Mr. Hartman attacked me, Julio. Nick saved me."

The man relaxed a little.

Nick motioned over his shoulder. "Can you lock him up someplace till we get the sheriff out here?"

Julio's grin lit the barn. "With great pleasure, señor."

Nick held onto Sierra and stormed toward the big, well-lit house on the hill. His knuckles hurt, and his face and ribs ached, but not half as much as Hartman's face. Nick was still so angry, it was a wonder he hadn't killed the man.

"Thank you," Sierra whispered, resting her head on his shoulder. "Thank you."

He felt her weeping and he hugged her a little tighter. "Shhh. It's all right now. He won't ever touch you again."

She sniffled. "I'm sorry to be a baby, but I have to admit he frightened me. He was going to teach me a lesson about obeying him."

"Reckon he's the one who got schooled."

She snorted a laugh through her sobs. "I dare say. And you didn't answer my question."

She looked up at him with glistening eyes so full of admiration that Nick faltered, but he had to get her inside and tended to.

"Why are you here?" she asked again. When he didn't answer, she started squirming in protest. "I'm all right. Put me down."

"You need a doctor."

"I need to know why you're here."

He huffed and then stopped and slowly set her on the ground, but he kept his arms around her. She kept her hands on his shoulders. Her gaze begged him for the truth, touched his soul, lit him on fire.

"I've got an extra ten thousand dollars. I hear you've got a pretty horse for sale."

Sierra laughed, but then flinched and touched one of the welts on her shoulder. Fully aware he could go back and kill the man who had done that to her, Nick drifted his fingers over the wound. Overwhelmed with a rush of mixed-up emotions, he pulled her into his arms and pressed his lips to the top of her head. "I came to ask you to forgive me…and I sure hope you will."

He wanted to say so much more, but he had no right, so he simply held her and waited. And prayed. "I'm so sorry," he whispered again.

Sierra swallowed and clutched him tighter. "You don't need pretty horses."

"Well, you know, I've been thinking about what you said. Shebar. He's fast, has a ton of endurance, and what a bloodline. All the way back to Sheik…Ali Baba."

"Sheik Moussaf El Adani."

"Yeah. Him." He lifted her chin so he could look at her. "I'm sorry about lying to you."

"I'm sorry for what my father did to yours, and the other ranchers. I didn't know."

"I figured that out…eventually. There were so many times I tried to tell you. That night in the library. And that day we rescued the calf. It's why I didn't kiss you."

"Did you want to?" She gazed up at him through long, alluring lashes that added a magical shimmer to her eyes.

He tried to read her face. In spite of what had just happened, she seemed to invite him to…to…

She raised her head a little, parted her lips.

Nick gave in to the temptation and brushed her lips. The touch of her mouth on his, the sweet feel of her body in his arms, the sheer relief of her safety, drove every rational thought from his brain. He gently deepened the kiss, and she responded, and he felt like the hero in a fairy tale.

His hand slipped down her satin back to the bustle, and the absurdity of the clothing brought his head up. "You always come to the barn dressed like that?" There was no way he could provide for a woman used to such things. Once more, he asked himself, what had he been thinking?

She looked down at her gown and sighed. "It cost a small herd."

"Well…" He didn't know what to say to that. He needed to get her some help. Needed to get on back to his own ranch, stop living in the fairy tale. He started to move with her, but she stopped him.

"And I'd gladly sell it. I'd gladly give up all this…for the right man."

He touched her cheek. "You'd be giving up an awful lot. More than you know."

"No. I'd be gaining more than I could ever tell you."

"Miss Sally said you'd make a good partner, and I knew she wasn't talking about business."

"I want to go back to Burning Dress. At least…for a little while."

Butterflies erupted in Nick's belly like a shotgun blast. "Would you…would you want to, you know, maybe let me court you?"

"With what intentions, sir?"

"Reckon I'd like to marry you, Miss Caldwell." Dang, he'd said it out loud. He hadn't planned on it, but there it was, and he was glad. *Lord, don't let her turn me down.*

She rose up on her tiptoes and kissed him. "How long do you think it will take you to get your ranch house livable?"

He grinned. "How fast can you say lickety-split?"

"Faster than you."

He chuckled, gave her a kiss on the nose, and they started walking to the big house on the hill. He had his arm around her, but was mindful of the welts. "Heck of a way to get engaged."

"Are you complaining?"

"Only about Hartman."

She hugged him tighter and he felt her shiver. "How did you find me? I didn't tell anyone I was at the barn."

He huffed a little laugh and leaned into her. "You know, Miss Sally said the strangest thing to me yesterday."

"What?"

"She said start with the stables."

"What?"

"Yeah, but then she waved it off. But when I rode up to your house, I thought of what she said...and it seemed the place to go."

Sierra shook her head, as if in awe. "Thank God for Miss Sally."

CHAPTER TWENTY-ONE

SALLY LIFTED THE LID ON THE LARGE CEDAR CHEST AND drifted her fingers over the pale-blue silk dress inside. It brought back so many wonderful memories and the smiling face of a little gal from Iowa.

"Oh, it's lovely," Sierra said, peering over her shoulder. "Is…is it yours?"

Sally smiled at the hesitation in the girl's voice. "No. It belonged to a young lady who was here for a time several years ago." She pulled the gown free from the chest and turned to Sierra. "She wished to donate it to a bride rather than burn it. Step over to the mirror and let's see how it looks."

Sierra gasped. "You mean I could—"

"Since your father has cut you off…" Sally let that drop and moved with the girl over to the full-length mirror in the corner. She draped it on Sierra's shoulders, and the two of them together held it in place.

"It's beautiful." Sierra brushed a hand down the pearl-studded bodice. Toile and silk intertwined in an elegant dance of pearls, embroidered flowers, and satin-covered buttons. "My. An expensive gown. Nice as anything I had to leave behind."

"Your father will come around," Sally said earnestly, meeting Sierra's eyes in the mirror. "And he'll kick himself for missing your wedding."

Sierra seemed to think things over for a moment. "Maybe, but it doesn't matter. I'm more concerned that he's so lost in his lust for power and money. I don't even know him anymore." She shivered. "And I was almost lost to that world, too." She laid a hand over Sally's. "Thank you."

"What did I do?"

"You built this place. Life is vibrant and real here. I found Jesus here. I found Nick here..." She shook her head, as if the right words eluded her. "It's a little bit of heaven on earth, I think."

Sally's heart warmed at the kind words. "It's my calling, and I love it."

Before Sierra could respond, someone knocked on Sally's door.

"It's Nick. Can I come in?"

Both women gasped and Sally quickly started folding the gown. "Just a moment." She tucked the dress back into the chest and closed the lid. "Sierra, we have a young lady here who is an excellent seamstress. If you like the gown, we'll have it tailored for you."

"Oh, that would be lovely."

"All right, then. Nick, come in."

He eased the door open and then smiled brightly at the women as he entered, motioning with his hat. "Maude told me Sierra was up here with you." He quickly stepped over and gave his bride-to-be a shy peck on the cheek.

The kiss was quick and awkward, but it still managed to work a blush from Sierra.

Amused by the bashful pair, Sally narrowed her eyes at the boy. "Everything all right?" It was, she knew, but something was percolating in the young man's brain.

Sierra took his hand and squeezed it. "You seem nervous."

Nick waved his hat. "It's more that I'm excited and a little befuddled. Something's happened."

"Well, quick, tell us," Sierra said, vibrating with curiosity.

"Walt from the livery came out to the ranch this morning and brought me this." He pulled a piece of paper from his vest pocket. "It's a telegram from your pa."

Sierra gasped and slowly took the paper from his hand. She opened it and read it. After a moment, she looked up at Sally. "My father said he's sorry he can't attend the wedding, but he would come for a visit soon. In the meantime, I have a present at the livery."

"Aw." Sally loved endings like this. *Thank You, Father.* "Do you have any idea what it is?"

Nick chuckled. "Walt told me. It's a big, beautiful palomino. A Morgan named Cleopatra."

"Oh," Sierra said with a gasp and fell into Nick's arms, her eyes wet with tears. "Cleopatra. He sent me Cleopatra."

A loving gaze, meant only for the couple, prompted Sally to clear her throat. "Why don't I leave you two alone for a moment?"

"You..." Sierra, her voice laced with tears, turned and gave Sally a tremulous smile. "You said he'd come around."

Sally shoved her hands in her pockets and gazed out

the window. "I tend not to give up on people. Long as they're breathing, there's a chance." She winked at the couple. "Take your time...but leave the door open."

Her steps light, her heart soaring, an angelic smile on her lips, Sally strode from the room.

THANK YOU

Thank you for reading *A Lost Heart*. I hope you loved this story as much as I do. If you have the time, I'd love if you could share a review on Amazon.

ABOUT THE AUTHOR

Heather Blanton is a *USA Today* bestselling author of thirty Christian Western romances, including the highly rated and awarded Romance in the Rockies series. She is also an award-winning script writer. Her Romance in the Rockies series has been optioned for a limited TV series, and her script *Unbridled Hearts* is currently optioned as well.

She grew up in the mountains of Western North Carolina on a steady diet of *Bonanza, Gunsmoke,* and John Wayne Westerns. Her daddy taught her to shoot when she was five, and she can hit that at which she aims.

Her novels are all Christian Western romance because she enjoys creating feisty pioneer women who struggle to find love and hold on to their faith. Like all good, old-fashioned Westerns, there is always justice, a moral message, American values, lots of high adventure, unexpected plot twists, and often a touch of suspense.

www.authorheatherblanton.com

www.ingramcontent.com/pod-product-compliance
Lightning Source LLC
LaVergne TN
LVHW040220110826
845146LV00005B/1346

* 9 7 9 8 8 9 5 6 7 8 4 2 8 *